PERDITA

FAITH GARDNER

MeritPress | fw

Published by
Merit Press
an imprint of F+W Media, Inc.
10151 Carver Road, Suite 200
Blue Ash, OH 45242. U.S.A.
www.meritpressbooks.com

ISBN 10: 1-4405-8811-2
ISBN 13: 978-1-4405-8811-2
eISBN 10: 1-4405-8812-0
eISBN 13: 978-1-4405-8812-9

Printed in the United States of America.

10   9   8   7   6   5   4   3   2   1

Library of Congress Cataloging-in-Publication Data
Gardner, Faith.
  Perdita / Faith Gardner.
    pages cm
  ISBN 978-1-4405-8811-2 (hc) -- ISBN 1-4405-8811-2 (hc) -- ISBN 978-1-4405-
8812-9 (ebook) -- ISBN 1-4405-8812-0 (ebook)
  [1. Death--Fiction. 2. Ghosts--Fiction.] I. Title.
  PZ7.1.G37Pe 2015
  [Fic]--dc23
                          2014047036

Cover design by Frank Rivera.
Cover and interior images © Sanhawut Panprapakorn/123RF.

This book is available at quantity discounts for bulk purchases.
For information, please call 1-800-289-0963.

CHAPTER 1

IS THIS SLEEP?

IT'S TWO WEEKS BEFORE JUNIOR YEAR STARTS and I don't know yet that I can see the dead.

Right now I'm not a ghost-seer. In fact, if you saw me, you'd probably guess I'm a professional slob, because I'm wearing a tank that's got a ketchup stain on the tit and some saggy yoga pants my sister doesn't want anymore. You'd watch me sitting here in my bedroom like some kind of bad-postured TV-zombie with my best friend Chloe (who, even in leggings and an '80s T-shirt with a faded surfboard on it, looks as if she could be a model for a skin or hair commercial), and you'd look back at me and think to yourself, "That girl? Pssh. Totally not special at all."

That's what I imagine people say when they see me, any-way. I mean, highlights of the moment would be the multiple empty bags of organic cheese puffs at my Freud-slippered feet (yeah, they're called "Freudian slippers," a gift from Mom—don't ask) and the fact that this is the sixth consecutive episode of a reality show about dead pets who come back to haunt people that Chloe and I have sat through without even moving to, like, adjust a bra strap or use the loo.

I should be appreciating the moment. You know, taking mental snapshots, basking in my ordinary existence. Doing those "mindfulness" exercises my mom does when she gets pissed at door-to-door solicitors or patients who won't stop calling her cell. But change gives no heads-up when it comes, earthquake-style, bumping and breaking loved but taken-for-granted things. So I spend the last few hours of normalcy watching a two-star reality TV show about the haunting of Smitty the cockatoo and a poltergeist that once was a cat named Mister Fluffers.

I've been laughing so hard I have quite possibly ruptured an ab muscle.

"Mister Fluffers," Chloe says again in her fake British accent. "'E was a fat old mangy beast of a cat, 'e was."

That's seriously how the gap-toothed Brit on TV talked about the poltergeist of her dead cat.

"She's crazy," I say, and then when I taste my own words, I stop to wonder. "I mean, right? You think these people are just nutcases—all of them?"

"They can't *all* be." Chloe pops a cheese puff in her mouth and chews it, thinking hard. "I mean, some are. The Mister Fluffers lady is off her gourd, obviously. But . . . ghosts have to exist in some form." She swallows. "Don't you think?"

I nod. Watching cheeseball shows about them is one thing. And I like that I can talk logically about them with Chloe, no biggie. But I'd never dare bring it up with my family. In this house, the concept just hits a little too near and a lot too sad. I believe in ghosts in secret. And—shhh, don't tell anyone—I still sleep with the lights on some nights, even though I'm old enough to have my driver's license.

"Cheer up," Chloe says, snapping her fingers in my face and squawking in her fake British accent again. "Don't let the thought of old Mister Fluffers get ya down."

"Stop," I giggle, and swat a cheese puff out of her hand.

The cheese puff flies across my room and disappears somewhere in the landfill of shoes and food packaging and now-meaningless school papers. This busts us both into tear-jerking laughter and we curl up on the bed in fetal positions, unable to speak.

Maybe I should warn you we did not sleep last night. As in, not a wink, so we're kind of a couple of delirious nutjobs. At a glance, you'd most likely assume we're high out of our minds. But please. In my house? Fat chance.

No, Chloe and I are just good, old-fashioned sleep-deprived.

Which is why, when my stick-up-a-butt sister Casey walks by my room with Perdita, Casey stops for a moment in the doorway to do what she does best: blab her unasked-for opinion.

"Wow," she says, eyeing both of us in our doubled-over positions on my bed. Also eyeing the mess on my floor. Casey's room looks as clean and minimal as a freaking museum. She organizes her socks by color. She uses a ruler to part her hair in the mornings. "You two *still* haven't gotten dressed?"

I sit up, correcting my posture, and Chloe does, too.

"Hey, we've got to live it up before the misery of school begins," I tell her.

"Don't be a such a hater," Casey says.

"Arielle's right," Perdita says behind her. She moves her platinum bangs out of her perfectly kohled-up eyes. "School sucks." Perdita is like a hundred times cooler than Casey, and it's still a mystery to me why she'd want to hang out with someone who's got a stick up her butt.

"You're just as bad," Casey says, turning to glare at her friend.

"Sorry we're not bluestockings bound for *Haaaa*rvard," Perdita jokes. "We're just good old working-class stiffs, right, girls?" She winks at us.

Casey huffs a sigh and leaves my doorway. Her ponytail follows her like a champagne-blond whip. Her hair is endless, past her butt, and she's kind of obsessed with it; her sprays and de-frizzers take up eighty percent of the cabinet space in the bathroom. But if I dare borrow a spritz of anything of hers she says I'm a "little klepto." For a *spritz*!

There is no sister in the world more annoying than my sister and, as rude as it may sound, I am so glad she's going to a fancy famous school in a week. Not because it's famous or fancy; 'cause it's on the other side of the country.

Perdita's still standing in the doorway, smiling at us with hot-pink lips, arms folded.

"What are you guys watching?" she asks.

"Show about dead pets that haunt people," I say.

"Oh my God, are you talking about *Phantom Animals: True Confessions*? I've seen every episode."

See? Why can't I have a sister like *that*?

"I haven't seen you lately," I say. "I thought you went away to school. Didn't Casey say you were going to San Francisco or something?"

"I was," Perdita answers, shrugging. "But . . . not anymore. Hey—did you know Tex is going to Velero High this year?"

Tex is Perdita's little brother, who went to Laguna Verde, a fancy private school in downtown Santa Katerina. I've kinda-sorta known him since we were in grade school together, plus the fact he lives a block away and our sisters were BFFs for years. But I haven't seen him in forever.

"Huh." I raise my eyebrows.

"Yeah, he was kicked out for straight Cs. Apparently he's not gifted and talented enough for the gifted and talented scholarship anymore." She laughs. "So now you get to deal with him. Make sure you give him shit for me."

"Okay," I say, even though, let's be honest: I'm not the type to give anyone shit.

"Later, ladies," she says.

She leaves, turning her back to us and showing off the rad patch sewn to the back of her leather jacket, of a fat red human heart—bloody and fist-shaped and crawling with veins and all. I hear my sister's door shut at the same time the doorbell rings downstairs. Soon footsteps thump up the stairs. My sister's friend Emily, who Chloe and I secretly joke is really a man (seriously, she's like six feet tall and all big-shouldered from swim team), walks by my room on her way to Casey's without even saying hi. That's how Emily is—if you're not eighteen-plus and on your way to an Ivy League, you don't exist. *Way* more my sister's type than Perdita, if you ask me. I guess that's why they're going off to Harvard together next week, and Perdita's staying behind. Casey and Perdita have been friends for almost as long as I can remember existing. Emily's more of a newer edition, my sister's new BFF as of a year or two ago.

"Perdita's such a badass," Chloe says, like she's telepathic, because best friends practically are.

"I know."

"I don't even know why she'd want to hang out with Casey and Emily."

"Perdita hasn't been hanging out as much."

"Shame, because she was the coolest thing about your sister."

"Duh."

"I wish I could pull off a leather jacket like that," Chloe says. "Even pleather looks wrong on me."

"Whatever. You could wear a garbage bag and people would gawk at you."

"Right, because I'd be wearing *a garbage bag.*"

"You know what I mean."

"It's called being a girl who's five-ten with big chee chees. Being curvy is its own curse."

I get tired of telling my best friend—the one who strangers often ask, "Do you model?"—how hot she is. Especially because I look like me. Not that I'm a dog or anything. It's just that I look like a teenage girl of sub-average height who gets pimples in her T-zone, must steal her sister's de-frizzers on occasion, and would need to hide balled-up socks in her bra in order to get a fraction of the eye-lust Chloe gets.

"You are very lucky," is all I can manage through my teeth at the moment.

"Right. Do you know how many awesome dresses I find at Trinkets that I can't even squeeze over my chest? It's heartbreaking."

Chloe works in downtown Velero at an antique store called Trinkets and Treasures, which aids her fabulous '60s-mod fashion sense.

"Yeah, my heart's just breaking for you and your huge tits," I say flatly.

She's about to protest, I'm sure, just as her phone buzzes. She glances at it. "Mom's here. Gotta run."

She stands and shoves her sparkly flats, yesterday's yellow dress, her paddle hairbrush, and *Anna Karenina* into her tote. On top of being drop-dead gorgeous, she's also an effortless genius. If she weren't my best friend in the whole wide world, I'd totally hate her.

"Bye," I say.

We squeeze a quick hug.

"Let me know the denouement of Mister Fluffers!" she exclaims in her British accent as she heads out my door.

I peek out my window, down at the front of our house, where her mom Trixie sits in her VW Bug. Trixie is like an older, tanner version of Chloe, and seriously the most laidback mom you could ask for. As in, she buys Chloe condoms "just in case"—even though Chloe hasn't had a boyfriend since ninth grade—and lets her drink wine with dinner. Chloe runs out to the car and jumps into the passenger seat. As the VW Bug makes a fast U-turn and chugs away, Chloe looks up at my window and sticks her tongue out at me.

All my deliriousness catches up with me in a hot second. It's only late afternoon, but I could pass out. I mute the TV and lie on my bed for a minute. When I close my eyes, remnants of that terrible show float into my brain-vision. I hear Chloe echoing "Mister Fluffers!" And, outside my crazy head, my sister's voice floats through the wall, mixing and overlapping with other voices, which is kind of extraordinary considering there's a bathroom separating us. I can only hear Casey when she's raising her voice. Which, apparently, she's doing right now.

Not that I'm proud of this, but I press my ear to the wall. It's an old trick. Little sisters are expert eavesdroppers. And anyway, if she doesn't want to be overheard, she shouldn't be yelling. But I'm too late. I hear Casey's door open, so I spring forward, away from the wall. A white-blond flash whizzes by my doorway and I hear heavy boots thud down the stairs, and then the slam of the front door. Capital-S *Slam*, a domestic sonic boom. I feel it in the floors. I mean, that's something Chloe would do, but Perdita? Cool as gelato.

I hang in my doorway, peeking down the hall at Casey's room. Casey's sniffing. As in, possibly even tears and weepy noises. Now I *know* something's wrong, because Casey is a desert. Even when we watched that depressing Holocaust movie last year, which made me bawl and nightmare for weeks, Casey just sat there dry-eyed and sighing. And now she's a faucet.

"Hey, guys?" I say, tiptoeing toward her door.

Emily just gets up and pushes the door closed and I hear the *snick* of the lock.

Alrighty then. Message received.

I'm so giddy-exhausted that the only comparison is that time last year when the dentist had me huff nitrous oxide before a filling. All I can really manage right now is walking downstairs and eating cold leftovers while slouching at the kitchen table. Which is what I do.

I sit there, staring at the vase of marbles that's the center-piece of the dining room table. I'm tasting barely anything, almost forgetting what I'm eating . . . oh yeah. Tuesday's cold spaghetti. Bleh. I rinse my bowl and space out as I stand in the dining room for a moment. That's when I see something gleaming on the carpet at the foot of the stairs. I swipe it and hold it up in the light. It's a necklace with a silver human heart on it. Like, a veiny human heart you see in bio textbooks—or the heart on the back of Perdita's jacket. The clasp is broken. It's unique and familiar. I'm sure I've seen it on Perdita before. She must have dropped it on her way out. Just for fun, I hold it up to my neck and catch a glimpse of myself in the small mirror that hangs next to our stairs in the entrance. I imagine what it would be like to be Perdita, to be one of the cool kids, fashion-able and bad in the best way.

Then it happens.

The feeling . . .

I can't explain it.

Everything shifts and becomes weirder than words.

Time warps for a second or maybe goes away entirely and then this . . . presence rolls in, kind of above me, also kind of behind me—wraps around me—an invisible body that fills the room. It's a wordless scream; *YOU ARE NOT ALONE*. It's someone standing right in back of me. And panic explodes, paralyzing me, like something really terrible is going to happen, or it's already happened and I'm reliving it. Devastating déjà vu.

And then I zero in on my eyes in the mirror. I can see it's just me. I can hear the tick of the clock behind me and see the table and the vase with the marbles in it again. I'm a little dizzy but the feeling lifts. The room empties and the moment is new again, and . . .

. . . I must be really tired.

Or it could have been a ghost, a whisper in me says, and I have to swallow hard and hold my breath for a minute to stop the shivers from rolling in. I turn and squint behind me, at the sliding glass door, at the darkening night, to make sure I don't see anyone.

"No ghosts," I whisper with a tight throat. "He's not here."

That's when I notice that Emily's standing at the top of the stairs with a weird expression in her eyes behind her tortoise-shell glasses.

"Are you . . . talking to yourself?" she asks.

"No," I say. Which, I realize, probably makes me look even crazier.

Emily just shakes her head and walks past me toward the door. As she leaves the house, I notice she has a fuzzy backpack shaped like a turtle, which elevates her to the status of Ultimate Dork.

I clearly need sleep. I wash my dish in the sink, wipe the counters, clean the microwave so Mom won't get all anal about it later. Before heading upstairs I go to the front door and pull on it to make sure it's locked, and it opens. I gasp and jump a few inches back when I see a figure crouching on the front porch. Then I realize it's Perdita. She's rooting around for something on the ground.

"Hey," she says, standing up. "Um . . . you haven't seen a necklace with a silver heart on it, have you?"

"You totally scared me," I say, hand on my chest.

"Sorry," she says. "I didn't want to . . . bug Casey about it. But I had it on when I was over earlier, I'm pretty sure. I just traced my steps back here and haven't found it."

"It's inside," I say. "Want to come in?"

"Um . . . that's okay. Can you just get it for me?"

"Sure, hold on." I turn around and grab it from the dining room table and hand it to her. "Yeah, it was at the foot of our stairs."

She breathes a sigh of relief. "*Thank* you. I was going crazy thinking I'd lost it. I haven't taken this necklace off since I got it three years ago." She holds it up in the porch light. "Fuck, it broke."

"Want a safety pin?" I ask.

"Yeah, that'd be awesome."

I go fetch her a safety pin from the kitchen drawer—I choose the hot-pink one because it seems to fit her—and come back to the front porch. She takes the safety pin and creates a makeshift clasp, hanging it back around her neck and fastening it. She squeezes the silver heart with relief.

"Thank you so much," she says again. "I was going to be so bummed. It was custom-made, so it's not like I can buy another one. I felt totally naked without it."

"No problem," I say.

"Have a good night," she says with a big hot-pink smile, still fondling her silver heart like she wants to make sure it'll never leave. "See ya around."

I close and lock the door and head upstairs. For a moment, I stand at the top of the stairs in the hallway, an aimless sadness flooding me. A week from now my sister's going to be gone. Not only that, my family's downsizing and moving across town in October, so soon I won't even have the comfort of my house, my room, the place I've known since I was born. I hesitate with my knuckles hovering over the gold star that says "Casey" on the door and then I knock quietly. Before I can knock a second time she's opened it and is staring—more like glaring, which is kind of her default expression when she's talking to me nowadays. Her eyes are a little pink but otherwise you'd never know she was just boo-hooing in here.

"Perdita just came by," I say. "She left her necklace here. I gave it back."

She puts her hands on her hips. "Good."

"Were you guys fighting?" I ask.

"How about you get a life of your own and stop bugging me about mine?"

Behind her, I can see she's already packing for next week. Her clothes are in folded, color-coordinated piles on the bed. She glances over her shoulder at her room and sighs.

"I'm just really busy. What do you want?"

"I had the weirdest feeling downstairs just now." At the mention of it my heartbeat gets a little flighty, like after a car almost veers into you or you nearly slice your finger on accident. "I imagined . . . a ghost or a spirit or something."

She speaks slowly, as if I'm two. "You felt a spirit."

"Maybe not. I was just scared. You know that feeling that you're not alone?"

There was a time when I could talk to my sister about these things—when I could run to her bedroom and she'd let me crawl under the covers when I got ridiculous and afraid. But over the past year or so, she's drifted and become meaner and less patient with me. I don't even know why I try to get her comfort anymore. Old habits die hard, I guess.

"*Okay,*" she says in a voice like I'm a nutcase.

"Never mind," I say.

"Are you hinting at Justin?" she asks in a low voice, looking behind me to make sure our parents aren't there to hear us.

"No," I say.

"Seriously, I don't have time to deal with your crazy imagination right now. Okay? Just . . . call Chloe or something." She shuts the door, like the rude human she is.

"I was just saying," I say.

"Whatever," I hear her mutter from inside her room.

"I can't wait 'til you go to stupid Harvard," I tell the gold paper star on her door.

"'Stupid Harvard' is an oxymoron."

I try to think of something clever to say, but the whole lack-of-sleep thing really doesn't leave me at the top of my game.

"You probably don't even know what an oxymoron is," she adds.

"Yes I do," I say.

I go back to my room and collapse on my bed. The sun set less than an hour ago, but I have to sleep. I shut my curtains and am getting under my covers when out of the corner of my eye, in the dim room, I see something.

A shape of a human being.

At first I think *Justin,* but then I blink and it changes.

It's dark—it's hard to make out exactly—but it looks like a skeleton girl.

The details are hazy, as if I'm watching something murky and underwater, or the blurry negative of a photograph. It's a skull with blond wig-like hair. Like one of those bony models you'd see in Bio, only right here, to the left of me, in the corner of my room. She's wearing a dark jacket, and beneath it— between the open zippers—I see a fire-red human heart behind the ribcage beating, beating, *beating.*

This is so familiar, this moment. That ghost? It's like I know her.

I want to reach for the light or scream. I can't. I'm paralyzed in bed. I know my wild imagination is practically famous. This isn't the first time I've seen things that aren't there, but this is scary, vivid, real.

The dark skeletal figure turns toward me, her eyeholes expanding so much that everything disappears into them, including me, and the room joins me in this blackness . . . unless . . . oh wait, maybe my eyes are shut and I'm falling down a dizzy quiet hole and . . . huh.

I don't know where I am right now.

Is this sleep?

CHAPTER 2
I WOULD HAVE WRITTEN IT DOWN

T HE NEXT MORNING, not-even-bright-yet and early, I wake up from the longest, deadest sleep. My head is pounding like I need water something fierce. I sit up in a haze and gulp down my entire glass that sits on my night table. Then I notice that my blankets and sheets are across the room, in the corner near my door. Which seems odd. I have to giggle, wondering what the hell I did in my sleep last night.

I rub my temples—they really hurt; I must be seriously dehydrated—and close my eyes, in a fog for a sec as I remember when I saw that *thing* that I don't even want to think about. It was undoubtedly a nightmare. I have nightmares sometimes when I'm falling asleep that feel crazy-real. Plus, I was spent. I slept like a corpse until dawn. I slept so solid my arms and legs hurt from whatever position I lay in. I go to the bathroom, gulp some Tylenol for my headache, and head downstairs. I snicker for a minute as I remember how freaked I was by absolutely nothing last night. Good thing I only told Casey, who brushed me off. My mom would have had something to say about it, and I'm sure whatever that something was would have been super annoying.

It's not easy having a shrink for a mom—she's rarely home, and when she is, she's got all sorts of theories about my behavior. Most if not every one of those theories often leads back to what I "could do better" and ways I "could improve." Fun stuff. Anyway, I could definitely improve my being a teenage scaredy-cat, apparently.

Enough. I'm going to grab an energy bar, put on my sneakers, and take a walk. I'm sore over *sleeping funny*; that's how out of shape I've become. School starts in less than two weeks and I'll bet I won't even be able to run a mile in under ten in PE, which is unacceptably pathetic.

It's not even six, so I'm the only one awake in the house when I step out the front door. The sun is turning the sky a gorgeous yellow-blue over the neighborhood. Lawns are empty; cars are parked in driveways; even the eucalyptuses across the street are dark and sleepy.

I live across the street from Lake Los Caballos, a hilly, tree-shrouded plot of land with what I'd call more of a glorified pond than a lake. It's lovely, surrounded by trails, hills, and tall grass, and I know every loop and turn. It's where Justin taught me to ride a bike, where Casey and I used to roller-skate, and where my dad used to take us to feed moldy bread to the dirty swans. I'm planning on walking there this morning when I notice the entrance, about half a block up, is flashing. Disco lights, I think at first. But as I walk nearer to it, my stomach sinks and my pulse bada-bumps: it's police lights. I get instantly queasy, like life just socked me in the gut.

The blinking red-blue of police lights always makes my stomach turn, ever since Justin died. I know it's been ten years, but some things never change. Like, for instance, death. And that's what this scene resembles: the lights, the crowd, squad cars parked and double-parked in the road. DEATH in capital letters.

It takes a gulp and whole lot of curiosity to make me go nearer and not run back into my house to hide in my bed. I mean, really, what could be happening? Nobody's *dead*. Maybe there was a fire (but where are the fire trucks?) or maybe a burglary happened (at the lake?) . . . okay, I have to know. I powerwalk closer and spot the yellow tape blocking off the entrance and the crowd—a dozen-ish neighbors, some with unbrushed hair and in sweats, like they've come running from their houses to look. And there's a van that has the words *CRIME SCENE UNIT* in black block letters on the side. And—yikes—another white van that just says, "Coroner."

Oh no, oh no, oh no.

My hometown of Velero, California, is a town with three freeway exits. It's actually a suburb of the fancier city of Santa Katerina, a hundred miles north of LA, where Hollywood celebrities buy second homes and *Fortune* 500 folks retire. Velero's not as fancy as Santa Katerina, but it's *nice*. It's safe. Our schools win awards. My parents don't lock their cars. Cops give tickets for jaywalking, that's how goody-goody this place is. In my sixteen years in this town I've never seen a crime scene unit van, or a coroner van, or police tape—not in real life, anyway.

On TV? In movies? Sure. Of course, I saw ambulances with Justin. That's why swirling red-blue lights make me want to puke. But that wasn't in Velero. And it wasn't a crime scene with tape and a coroner's van and all that. Although I have to say, right now, the screw grinding sickly in my stomach feels very much the same.

But this scene, a frenzy of flashing lights and bystanders across the street and down a few houses from my home, is crazytown. I join the crowd and try to peek between everyone's heads and over the yellow police tape. All I can see are cops gesturing, talking.

"What's going on?" I ask Mrs. Danvers, a woman from up the street who's always losing her ADD dog and knocking on doors with a leash in her hand.

She squints at me. She clutches a rolled-up newspaper, as if she was walking out to grab it and got distracted by the scene. "They found a body," she says quietly. "That's what they're saying."

"Here?" I squeak. "Who?"

"A girl drowned," a man with a comb-over who I recognize from the neighborhood butts in. "I heard them saying that a girl drowned."

When he says that word, *drowned*, it's like someone pushed me off a cliff.

"My daughter's in the house, thank God," a frizzy-haired woman says. She looks ready to burst into tears.

Drowned echoes through me and sends my blood into a panic.

Stop it. Calm down. That was then; this is now. There's no way it's Casey. Remember, self? You heard her snoring while getting Tylenol from the bathroom. And Chloe lives too far away for it to be Chloe. The people I love are safe. But still. Hairs are standing up on my arms, and it's sixty-five degrees outside.

A man standing next to me tries to flag down one of the nearby police officers for the skinny, but the officer just says, "Everyone, please stay back."

I almost think about calling Chloe, but she sleeps 'til noon if she has no reason to get out of bed. And I know telling my family would only upset them and unleash the flashbacks.

This crowd is full of tall worriers and I can't see a thing. So I backtrack in the direction I just came from—twenty feet or so away from the entrance—and climb into the brush, getting stickers all over my legs and arms, hoping to get a better view. I am so sick as I watch, and yet I can't look away.

From here I can see the action. I can see the steep cement bank that drops into the lake and read the "NO SWIM-MING" sign; I can see the expressions on the officers' faces—determined, puzzled—and the gurney waiting next to the bank. I draw in a sharp breath, imagining Justin's lifeless body being strapped to it—stop it, brain, stop. This is different.

A couple people with polo shirts that read "CRIME SCENE UNIT" and someone in plain clothes, with a badge hanging around his neck, stand in the water up to their shins. That's when I see it there, floating, beside them.

"It"—what am I saying? She's quite clearly a "her."

Or, I mean, *was* a her.

The corpse resembles a mannequin floating face down in the murk.

I gasp and clutch a tree branch for support. I taste puke in my throat and swallow hard, close my eyes, and then will them open again. The tree branch is ant-swarmed, so I pull my hand away and swat at my arm as I keep spying on the scene and remind myself to breathe. I crawl over a few bushes to get closer—I'm hidden in oaks and shadows, so there's no way anyone can see me at this point, from inside or outside the lake. But I can see everything.

And when they pull her bloated, discolored body from the water and lay her on the gurney, her wet platinum hair falling stringy, her face with clouded, open eyes falling my way as if she's looking right at me, I recognize her. I hear people in the crowd gasp and break into murmurs, too. We all seem to recognize her at once.

My skin pales fast. I don't need a mirror to verify. I feel like I just lost a quart of blood. My eyes hurt with tears and I start whispering, "No, please, please, no . . ."

It's Perdita Dell.

I clamp my hand over my mouth and start crying. It's Perdita. I know it's Perdita—I just stared at her face like twelve hours ago! I even recognize the cheetah-print dress she's wearing and her leather boots. My mouth hangs open and I can taste my tears. This horror is so familiar—to stumble upon a scene of panic and death, and to recognize the dead person as someone you know—it's beyond nightmarish. It's so terrible it's unreal.

I can hear a mix of talk through the bushes, to the left of me, where everyone buzzes with information for the cops.

"It's the Dells' daughter . . ."

"She lives around the block. I can show you, officer . . ."

"Perdita's her name—I think she's in high school . . ."

"So sad . . ."

"Looks like an accident, the way the water drops off there . . ."

"We need a fence up here to prevent these kinds of tragedies . . ."

"I've heard that kids do drugs here after it closes. It's dangerous . . ."

"Yeah, I've seen beer cans and litter around here. It's not safe . . ."

"So dark at night . . ."

Meanwhile a photographer in one of those CRIME SCENE UNIT polos snaps pictures of Perdita, lifts her arms while the detective guy jots notes in a black book, not crying, not realizing this was a girl who graduated only months ago and whose life was supposed to be just beginning. This was a girl who was never mean to anyone, who gave me rides places when I needed them sometimes, who always poked her head in my door and asked me how I was doing and, unlike my own sister, treated me like a person who deserved to be listened to. And all I can think is, *Casey*. Casey's brother and best friend of many years, both drowned. What are the odds? In *Velero*? This is going to be so traumatic.

I have to bite my own tongue to double-check I'm not nightmaring.

It's when they bust out the bright-blue body bag and put Perdita inside it and zip it up over her boots, her legs, her torso, that I know this is pinch-me real. I've never seen a body bag in real life before. With Justin, they just draped a blanket over him and put him on a gurney. Perdita's face is turned my way, stiff half-open lips, violet-blue tinge to her skin, some hair mashed wet against her cheek, and soon that too disappears into the crayon-sky-blue bag, zipped up like the saddest unspoken goodbye you never heard. They wheel her bagged body on the gurney up the trail that leads away from the cement bank. That sound—those wheels creaking—it's been ten years but I still remember. I hear a cop telling people to clear the way. I sit there, on a stump, with my head in my hands for a long time, stunned and stop-and-start crying. I emerge from the bushes and turn in the opposite direction from the vans, cop cars, and flashing lights. I cross the street to my house and stand, stumped, on my own doorstep. This is where Perdita stood yesterday, fastening her necklace back on. This has surpassed unreal. And now I have to go inside and break the news to my family—I've never had to do something like that; I don't know how! I don't know if any of us have even uttered the word *drown* in years. It's just—it's a word we avoid. This is going to bring it all up again. I dab my tears with my fingers and try to catch my breath to go inside. The lights are on in the window. Everyone's up. I wish I could just disappear.

The body bag, bright blue, her lifeless face—even from so many feet away it was obvious who she was and that she was very, very dead. It was the same way with Justin. The moment all the kids at camp went running to the shore, I recognized my big brother from forty feet back and I knew he was no longer alive, no matter how much the camp counselor huffed and puffed with mouth-to-mouth. Casey shrieking and pulling her hair and my heart swelling too big for my body. With Perdita, she didn't even have a chance—it was beyond late. No CPR, no fighting chance, no ambulance. When, then, did Perdita die? Early this morning? Late last night? Right after she ran out of our house? Did she slip and fall? Was she drunk and stoned like the people I overheard were implying?

God, why did I have to see that thing I will never be able to un-see?

I don't know if I can hold down that energy bar. I want to go back to bed and shut my eyes and wake up again and find out none of this has been real. I want to go back.

But I know, as I put my hand on the front doorknob, that's an impossible wish. I know well what death means. We never get to go back to the way things were before. Deep breath, Arielle.

I push open the door.

Casey doesn't shed a tear when I break the news as she eats her oatmeal at the kitchen table. She looks stung, offended, like someone slapped. Then she rolls her eyes and shakes her head and acts as if I've invented the whopper to end all whoppers.

"That's a disgusting thing to say," she says. "Why would you even *say* that?"

Her hair is in a long wet braid and her face shines with cream. Dad, who's got no mannequins to dress at the moment (yeah, that's what he does for a living these days), turns around with a peeled banana in his hand.

"*What* did you just say?" he asks me through a mouthful of banana. He swallows like it hurts. And I don't need psychic powers to know what they're both thinking, because I'm thinking it, too. You don't mention the word *drowned* without that blank space Justin occupies suddenly washing over us and spreading a thick, unspoken sadness.

"I saw her," I say, more to Casey than to him. "I mean, open your freaking eyes and look out the window—there's still cops there and the crime scene tape—"

Casey jumps up, scrapes her chair back with a screech, and she and my father head to the front of the house. I hear the curtains being parted and then the front door opening and footsteps running.

My dad comes back, alone.

"Arielle . . . are you sure?" he asks, his color instantly whiter as he stands with the banana in his hand like he doesn't know what to do with it anymore.

"It was Perdita," I say, voice shaking. "I'm not lying."

He puts the banana on the counter. "But kiddo—how do you know it was her?"

"Dad, I *saw* her. I know her; I saw her. Everyone in the crowd recognized her, too."

"No—I just can't . . . oh my God." His mouth hangs open and I watch the news becoming real in his face. I watch the pain in remembering. "Oh my God, no . . ."

He hugs me and doesn't let me go for a long time.

Casey comes back, pale as a dinner plate.

"Perdita," she says. And then she drops the final word. "Drowned."

I wait for her to cry. But first, she goes to the kitchen sink and starts throwing up oatmeal.

Mom comes home early from work, which is unheard of. Apparently someone has to die in order for her to cancel appointments with clients. The four of us—parents, Casey, and I sit in the living room together, the three of them on the couch, me on the ottoman.

"I can't believe she was just here yesterday," my mom says, as if existence yesterday can logically undo death today. She wipes at her eyes with a tissue before tears can escape and leave marks.

When my mother cries, her face doesn't change expression—tears just fall from her otherwise normal-looking eyes. Polar opposite of my father, who weeps like a banshee and usually even does some dramatic gesture to accompany it—chest-clutching, hand-wringing. After Justin died, I became all too familiar with everyone's crying techniques. And then there's Casey, who more resembles someone who was slugged in the stomach and can't breathe right than a teenage girl who's lost her once-closest friend.

"Why was there crime scene tape and detectives?" I ask. "It didn't seem like there was a crime. I don't get it."

"Crime scene tape just means they're sectioning the area off; they do that for suicides or accidents sometimes," Mom says.

"They send out people to investigate if they don't know the cause of death," Dad says. "Just to make sure."

"Everyone was saying it was an accident," I say. "They said that's where kids partied."

My mom shakes her head. "Such a shame."

"I can't . . . I can't believe this." Casey's stuck in those four words. "I can't believe this."

"I'm so sorry, honey. I'm so sorry." Dad's face wrenches up. He buries his head in his hands and weeps. Loudly. I know what he's thinking. Justin's not-hereness is so big it fills the room. He had been twelve. Talk about your whole life being ahead of you. He hadn't even graduated junior high.

"We had a fight yesterday," Casey says so quietly it could pass as a whisper. "I hadn't even seen her in weeks. She was supposed to go to SF State and yesterday she told me she dropped her classes and was staying in Velero." Casey's face screws up and she takes a quaky breath. "I told her I was disappointed in her. I feel so bad . . . we weren't that close lately . . . we were just . . . we were different."

"She did seem different," my mom says, rubbing Casey's arm. "She dressed more 'goth' or whatever you kids call it."

"She wasn't goth, Mom," I cut in.

"Yeah—that's not goth," Casey says.

"Well, you know what I mean. The heavy boots, the leather jacket, the white hair."

"That's not goth?" Dad asks, wiping his tearstained face. "Is it punk, is that what that is?"

"I don't know," Casey says, her voice rising a little. "It was just her style."

"Was she into . . . I don't know, bad things?" my mom asks.

Casey watches the carpet as if it holds all of life's answers. "We just . . . drifted apart."

"Was she on dope or something?" Dad asks.

Yeah, my dad says stuff like "on dope," too.

"I don't know what she was into," Casey says. "She didn't talk to me about things anymore."

I almost think she's going to cry, but instead Casey shuts her eyes for a minute like they burn.

"I'm supposed to go to Cambridge in less than a week," she says, eyes still shut. "How am I supposed to be able to do that?"

"You could just not go," I say.

She stares at me, pink-eyed and tired. "*Why?* What good would that do?"

"Your best friend *died*," I tell her.

"Arielle," my mom says, as if my mentioning it was in bad taste.

Was it? I mean, she's dead. It's a fact: I just saw her body with my own eyes.

"You worked so hard for this," Dad says to Casey. "You have to go."

"The funeral will probably be in a few days," Mom says. "You'll be able to make it in time for classes."

"Maybe it'll even be good for you to get away from it, have something to focus on," Dad says.

Casey nods and studies her pajama pants, which are covered in little cartoon owls. "I'll go," she says.

Mom and Dad head upstairs and Casey follows. After a silent, cold minute I follow Casey upstairs, too. I can't believe she cares about stupid Harvard right now—if Chloe was dead, I'd be mourning for months. But Casey seems to be on autopilot. I see her in her room, ogling her open suitcases on the floor. She looks up at me with a faraway expression. I wish I knew how to comfort my sister.

"Um, hi," she says. "Can I help you?"

"I'm just in shock," I say.

"*You're* in shock."

I tiptoe to her doorway and hang there for a minute, staring at her boring black-and-white photos on her wall of rainy streets and wet roses. Her fingers twist her long blond braid and she keeps swallowing.

"I'm really sorry," I say.

She nods.

"This has been such an unreal day," I say. "I mean, since last night, I've felt like I'm dreaming. That ghost."

"God, you are *so* self-absorbed," she says, lips a hard line and eyes tiny with rage. "This isn't about you! Ever thought of that?

That maybe all of this has nothing to do with you? Oh, no, you didn't—because you're *Arielle*."

My neck gets hot and itchy the way it does when I'm humiliated. "I was just saying."

"My friend died," she yells. "My *friend* is *dead*."

"I saw her being dragged out of the water!" I yell back, everything getting blurry with my tears. Don't cry! I beg myself. That's no way to get Casey to listen. But it's too late. My tears have always been disobedient troublemakers.

"So what? She's *my* best friend!"

"It affects me, too!"

Now my parents' door opens and my dad comes out. He's in his boxers.

"Girls—"

"Dad, Arielle's such a self-centered b—"

"Casey, I hate you—"

"Okay, this is a very emotional day; tensions are running high," Dad says, putting his hands out in a referee gesture.

I wipe my face. "I can't wait until you go," I tell Casey.

"You know what? I can't wait to go, either!" And—lo and behold—a tear springs from her eye.

I go to my room and slam the door. Then I stand there, listening. I hear my mom's voice join the conversation.

"It's not about her!" Casey is crying. "Why does she make everything about her?"

I expect my mom to tell Casey she's right, since Mom tends to side with Casey on pretty much everything, but my mom actually defends me, to my surprise.

"This is hard on all of us," Mom says. "Hardest on you, of course, honey. But Arielle witnessed it. And it brings up a lot of bad memories. You know?"

"She *saw* the body today," Dad adds. "She's probably—she's probably processing a lot right now."

"And I'm *not*?" snivels Casey.

"She's only sixteen and she's more emotional than you. Cut her some slack," Mom says.

"She's also a liar," Casey says. "She exaggerates to get attention—"

"Casey," Dad says. "You're getting yourself worked up over the wrong things here. Why don't you take a bath and relax, okay? Lie down or something. Just—calm down. Who cares about Arielle right now?"

That last sentence floods me with a new emotional cocktail—a mix of relief and sadness. Who cares about me? Who cares?

I flop on my bed and start crying. Not loud like an actor, the way my dad cries. Not tearless like Casey. I heave near-silent sobs and hug my pillow, wishing this whole day never happened, wishing the thought of my dead brother would leave me alone, remembering yesterday when Perdita stood on the porch with me—what was the last thing she said?

I can't even remember now. It's gone. I might as well have made it up inside my head.

It reminds me of Justin. I had seen him at the cafeteria at camp at breakfast. He said something to me when he walked by, teased me, called me some silly name, and yanked my pigtail. I don't remember his words now. I just remember his red baseball cap and his freckles. But if someone had told me it would be the last time I'd see him alive, I would have written it down.

CHAPTER 3
MOONLESS WORLD WITH NO STARS

THE GARDENS OUTSIDE THIS PLACE are filled with fuchsia flowers and crawling vines; the trees glow in the gold haze of the afternoon sun—it would be gorgeous if it weren't, you know, a funeral home. It's weird how I've passed this Spanish-style building so many times before on the bus on the way to the mall, but it wasn't until right now that I realized what it was. We walk quietly up the steps in shiny shoes. Dad's in a suit—I didn't even know he owned one, to be honest. Mom's in a black pantsuit, holding a sympathy card we all picked out together at the drugstore on the way. Chloe's hand is gripping my hand as we head through the open door. I'm so glad she came. I know I sound selfish, but I really don't want to go inside—I've never been to a wake before. With Justin, he was cremated and we had a memorial service with just family the day we sprinkled his ashes in the ocean. My mom explained in the car that we're going to see Perdita's body again, and there are nasty butterflies aflutter in my belly.

"It's going to be okay," Chloe whispers as we walk through the entrance.

I nod, pretending I'm strong, when really I wish I could shrink right now into something atomic and invisible.

Inside the white-walled building with paisley carpets, a man in a suit greets us and points to the left. We walk in and it seems every chair in the room is filled. I've never seen so much black fabric in one building. Velero's a not-huge town, like twentysomethingthousand people. But I swear half the population has shown up today. There's a string quartet in the corner playing some sad song that immediately threatens to choke me up. Yet I imagine if Perdita were here she'd say something like, "Oh God, how totally boring. I can't believe they have a freaking *cello* here. What century do they think it is?"

In the second row back, I spot my sister, who's been here since the wake started. Emily, in a flowery dress and what looks like a fisherman's hat, is sitting next to her. I spot a guy with slicked-back hair sitting near them who I'm pretty sure is Perdita's boyfriend, or was last year, anyway. His name's Raffi. He's a boxer and, according to the general consensus among the female population at school, a dreamboat. In the front row, I can see the Dells—or, at least, Perdita's parents. I recognize that signature poof of bleached-blond hair that belongs to her mother and the shiny-bald head of her father. I don't see her brother anywhere. When I glance up front, where the flowers are, my heart seems to stop pumping for a sec. She's across the room, but I can see her profile and her red, red lips. Perdita's as white as the coffin she lies in.

"She looks so pretty," Chloe whispers.

I stare at the carpet, at my shiny shoes, and don't respond. Because I don't really agree. Perdita looks stranger than a stranger. She's a mannequin; she's a skeleton in a dress.

I shiver, remembering that nightmare I had.

"It's amazing what they can do," Chloe whispers. "I mean, how nice they can make her look."

Really? I want to say. I mean, sure, she looks nothing like the bruise-colored girl they pulled from the lake days ago and zipped up in blue. But she doesn't look like Perdita, either. Her skin is colorless and not-human-looking. Then there's the fact she's wearing a pale-pink dress and some pearls. She would so hate that. "They're sending me off to eternity looking like a total dweeb!" I imagine her saying.

"You want to get in line to pay your respects?" Mom leans over to ask me.

"Pay my . . ." I look ahead, at the line of people waiting to walk up to the coffin.

Oh God.

Do I have to?

Is that mandatory?

"We're going up there," Mom says. "Ready?"

Dad's blowing his nose in a hanky. He's probably already gone through five of them and we just got here.

"I'll just . . . wait here," Chloe says, squeezing my hand and letting go. "Let you do your thing."

I follow my parents to the line even though I would rather hide underneath a chair. We nod at my sister, who looks up at us from her seat. Her expression is so blank and faraway I almost wonder if she doesn't recognize us for a second. Finally, she nods back. Emily waves at us from her seat. Her fuzzy turtle backpack is at her feet. Even at a funeral.

One by one, people go up to the coffin and whisper things or make the sign of the cross. I'm not sure what to do, what to say. What do you say to a dead body? What's the point? Is it like the times when I was a kid and I would talk to Justin late at night, in bed, imagining his ghost hanging around to listen to me as if he was some kind of therapist? I don't know the rules for these sorts of things. I look back and Chloe is glancing at her phone—which seems tacky, but no one appears to notice. My parents go up before me. Dad snivels into his hanky. Mom says a few quiet words with her hands folded in front of her. When they're done, they go over to Perdita's parents. I stand here, stuck at the front of the line, paralyzed, not wanting to go forward. It's like that time I went to Magic Mountain and waited in line to go on Superman and then, once it was time to get into the car, every cell in my body screamed NO and wouldn't move. I chickened out. But that's not an option now, Arielle—you're sixteen and this isn't a freaking roller coaster. Just go up and say goodbye. It's not that hard. Everyone else here is doing it. People are waiting behind you.

I force my feet to make steps toward the coffin. Closer, closer, until Perdita—or this body that once held Perdita—is an arm's length in front of me. Her face looks more bloated than it looked in real life, her hair thinner. The makeup is cakey, like a stage actress's. I stare at her closed eyes and the almost-smile on her still-red lips, expecting her to start choking, her lids to flap open, for her to sit upright and spit pebbled sand and gurgle, "I'm still here! Don't forget me!"

I see her in the water again, the way her head fell to the side and she seemed to look at me with dead eyes.

I suck in air. My mouth opens, but no sound comes out. I am totally and completely stuck. My hands start shaking and I back up—I can't stop myself, my body's on autopilot—and I head back the way I came. I pass the line of people waiting. I pass the people in chairs, I pass Chloe, and I go out the door into the lobby area where we entered. I think I might be sick.

"Bathroom?" I ask the man standing at the front door.

"Outside, around the corner to the left," he says. "Before the garden."

"Thanks."

I hope I make it that far. I hurry my heels out the door, down the steps, run past the pretty fuchsia and the crawling vines, and follow the terra cotta tiles around the corner. Inside the ladies' room, I lock the door. I stand over the sink. My ears ring. Whoa—in the mirror's reflection, I look as white as Perdita. I'm trembling. I feel terrible, so guilty for running out of there like a wuss. I start crying and lean against the wall for a second, wipe my eyes frantically so mascara doesn't river down my face. After a few minutes, I catch my breath and my hands stop shaking. My stomach settles. I dab some water on my cheeks, which seem to have some color in them again.

I go outside. The sunset is cotton candy, clouds stretched and pink. I wonder, is it for her? Can a ghost influence a sunset? That's when I smell something . . . skunky. Smoky. I know right away what that smell is; I just can't believe my nose because, you know, I'm at a *funeral home*.

It's coming from the back. I follow the smell past the men's room, where the terra cotta tiles turn left into a courtyard. There's a bench between two oaks that faces a garden filled with more hot-pink foliage and creeping ivy. A shaggy-haired guy in a button-up shirt has his back to me. His tie, black, is balled up next to him. He's staring at the sunset above the garden and I'm guessing he's responsible for the pot smell, since no one else is around. What a disrespectful asshole, I think. I'm about to turn around to sneak away, but he whips around and sees me first.

"Oh," we both say, startled by the sight of each other.

It's Tex, Perdita's brother. Last time I saw him he had a buzzed head, so I didn't recognize the hair. He's got stubble on his chin now. I realize how long it must have been since I saw him, because he looks older, almost like someone else.

"Hey, Arielle," he says.

"Hi."

We stare for a minute. His eyes are kind of pink—from crying? From weed? I don't know. I'm guessing now's not the most appropriate time to ask him.

"Why are you out here?" I ask.

He shrugs. "I don't want to be in there." He doesn't blink or change expression. I wonder what's going on in there. I feel so bad for him, his family, everyone. "You?"

"I wasn't feeling well," I say. "I don't know."

"Me, neither," he says.

He turns back around and faces the sunset again.

I don't know the proper thing to say to him. Should I leave him alone? He seems like he wants to be left alone. I start to turn around to head back to the wake but then rethink it. Nobody ever gets offended by showing you care, by showing you're sorry, I tell myself. I walk back over to him and stand next to the bench.

"Can I sit with you?" I ask softly.

"I guess," he says, looking up. He grabs his tie and tosses it on top of his jacket on the ground.

I sit next to him, on the end of the bench to give him space.

"I'm really sorry," I say.

"Thanks," he says, like he's heard it before, which I'm sure he has. Probably a thousand times today, in fact. Sorries don't exactly help. So I stare ahead at the pink sky.

"I hear you're going to Velero High," I tell him.

"Who told you that?" he asks.

"Perdita, actually."

He turns, surprised.

"Last time she was over," I say. "She said to give you shit for her when I see you."

He snorts. His face actually changes—some life is breathed into him for a second. "Yeah, that sounds like what she'd say."

I have a hard time not gawking at his face right now, because Perdita's there. Perdita's eyes are shaped like his, their color even the same blue-green with yellow in the middle. It's hard not to see her in him. I wonder if he looks in the mirror and sees that, too, and if it's hard, or if it's comforting. I was too young to think about things like that when Justin died.

"Maybe we'll have a class together and I can be sure to give you some shit then," I say, hoping to make him laugh.

But a shadow seems to have crossed his expression and all he says is, "Yeah."

In a tree in front of us, a bird cries and another bird answers it.

"Were you smoking weed?" I whisper.

"Who cares?" he answers after a pause.

I shouldn't have asked. It just kind of blurted itself out. I mean, really, in the big picture today, whether or not he just got high seems pretty insignificant.

"Sorry," I say. "You're totally right."

"You were the D.A.R.E. girl," he says. "You haven't changed, huh?"

For a second I stare at him, having no idea what he means by "dare girl." But then I realize he means the D.A.R.E. program, which he and I had to go through in sixth grade together. I won an award for giving an impassioned speech about how terrible drugs are when I was eleven. It seems stupid now. Actually, I totally forgot that it ever happened until this moment.

I laugh. "Oh yeah!"

"Yeah," he says. "What a nerd."

"We were eleven," I say. "And excuse me, *I* wasn't a brainiac who got into Laguna Verde on scholarship. Talk about nerds."

He smiles and stares at his hands.

"How are your parents doing?" I ask.

"They're just what you'd expect—total wrecks," Tex says.

I nod. "Of course."

"The cops are trying to say it was an accident, she was drunk or high or something. My mom's convinced they're wrong. She acts like there's an answer, like, I don't know, the cops aren't doing their job. She keeps grasping for a why."

He gently flexes his hand into a fist and touches his own knuckles, one by one.

"I think that's just what people do when . . . something like this happens," I say, remembering how my mother was when Justin died—convinced he had eaten too soon before getting into the lake, that he had slipped and fallen, that the camp counselors hadn't done CPR right, that there was some explanation. He was a good swimmer. It seemed impossible. But gradually she stopped talking about answers. We all did.

"Yeah," he says. "Probably. They say we'll know for sure in a couple weeks; they're running some report or something. Maybe then my mom'll finally accept it."

I want to tell him the truth—that a part of you never accepts it. A part of you walks the world still seeing that person in strangers (little freckled boys in red baseball caps, for instance), and lies awake at night wondering if that chill you feel is his ghost. You only accept it on the surface. Your heart, it never learns.

"Yeah," I say instead.

I can't remember the last time I talked to Tex—that Fourth of July barbeque a couple years ago that both our families went to? I swear we said about two sentences to each other and then broke off to do our separate things. That time I saw him at the mall and we didn't even say hi? I've never been close to him or anything; he's just kind of been . . . around. But right now it's almost as if I'm really seeing him for the first time. We're grown up and we have something real to talk about. It's amazing how in five minutes, you can warm to someone. It only takes a conversation to make someone something like a friend.

"Well," I say, getting up. "I should go find my parents."

"Cool," he says, and nods. "Thanks for stopping by."

"I'll see you at school?"

"School," he sighs. "Oh yeah. I guess so."

Our eyes lock. There are immeasurable worlds of sadness there. Poor guy. I want to hug him, but that seems too weird.

"Listen, if you ever want to talk . . . " I say.

I want to tell him I understand. I understand what you're feeling more than you know. I want to say, I had a brother once; did you know that? And I lost him the same way. But the words just don't come from my stubborn lips.

"Sure," he says.

He doesn't believe me. He thinks I'm just saying that to make him feel better. Can I blame him? Surely I'm not the first or last person to say that today. His sadness and bitterness are walls I can't climb right now. And it's not like I should expect any more, when his sister's not even buried yet.

"See you around," I say.

He gives me a little wave as I leave, and then turns back around, slumped, to stare at the sun, which is sinking behind the purple hills.

That night, in bed, I'm dizzy with tired. I can hear Casey on the phone down the hall. Not what she's saying or anything, just the drone of her voice. She sounds monotone. She's probably talking to Emily again. If she's not with Emily lately, she's talking to her on the phone. Which I guess is good for her. She needs a friend. Casey's looked sick and strange these past few days, like someone vacuumed her spirit away.

Perdita could be underground by now. I don't know how that works; we only attended the wake for a half-hour and then came straight home. Truth be told, I don't even know where a cemetery is in this town; that's how ignorant I am. In the dark, under the covers, I try to think about other things—my class schedule for next semester, what I'm going to wear the first day of school, whether or not I should try to get my license. But instead, other thoughts take over. I imagine Justin, and fire, and how sadly light the cardboard box was that held his ashes. The way his ashes hit the ocean with the quietest *pat* like fish food and sank. I imagine the coffin lid closing over Perdita's white, skeletal face, and the coffin being lowered into the cold, damp earth . . . gulp. My heart beats madly. I turn to my left, where I saw the skeleton girl in that nightmare I had. It's emptiness now. It's all emptiness, this feeling, the say-nothing of the night—emptiness so big it has no words. Looking up at my open window where crickets hum and highways sing, I drink the darkness in with my eyes.

"Perdita," I say, like the night and she have something in common.

But no. Wherever she's gone, it's a moonless world with no stars.

CHAPTER 4
A KNOCKING THAT WON'T GO AWAY

THE DAY CASEY LEAVES FOR MASSACHUSETTS, Mom takes the day off work, which for her is a really big deal. Dad makes Casey's favorite breakfast—blintzes. Because of course my sister's food of choice has to be obscure and impossible to make. Me? Bacon and scrambled eggs would do me just fine. Plus, I'll be honest: I don't even know for sure what a blintz is.

"They're Russian," Casey tells me.

"Good for them," I say.

I guess I should just be glad Casey's eating. She's probably lost ten pounds since Perdita died. Her collarbones stick out; her cheekbones are obvious.

"My baby girl, my first baby girl." Mom watches Casey pick at the blintz Dad just plopped on her plate. It looks like a mini-burrito slathered with jam—gag.

"I'll just have cereal," I say, getting up for the box.

Even though Mom's not a crier, her eyes are extra shiny behind her glasses. She's got one pair of reading glasses perched on her nose and an identical pair perched on her head. There's a magazine with a picture of a brain on it in front of her, unopened, and a cup of coffee: my mother doesn't believe in solid breakfasts.

"How are you feeling?" Mom asks Casey.

Casey chews and swallows before answering. "I haven't slept a full night in days. I just—I hope I can concentrate once I get there."

"It'll feel good to be somewhere new," Mom says. "You'll be able to leave all this behind and focus on school. I've never known you to have trouble in school, even when . . ."

. . . *even when Justin died* is what she means. But Mom pauses and swallows coffee before finishing her sentence.

"Even when you're under stress," she says.

Which is true. After the summer Justin died, Casey went into fourth grade and became class secretary and kicked serious butt in soccer that year. Me? I started wetting the bed again and had to get counseling because I drew pictures of ghosts and burning people during free time. As Mom says, we all mourn in our own way.

"You have that pepper spray I gave you, right?" Dad asks, sitting down at the table with a plate of ugly, reject-looking blintzes. He gave Casey the pretty ones.

"Yes, Dad," Casey says.

"And we're paying for that phone, so we expect phone calls. Regularly," Mom says.

"Of course."

I chomp my cereal and stare at the vase of marbles. I look behind me at the clock: only a couple hours until Casey's plane leaves. Crazy. Even though she and I haven't exactly been buddies lately, I can't imagine this house without her. And soon, we won't even be in this house—we'll be somewhere new. Why does change have to be a flood and not a drizzle?

"What about you, kiddo?" Dad asks me.

"I don't know," I say. "What do you mean?"

"Well, you're going to be an only child pretty soon," Dad says.

It sounds so sad when he puts it that way.

"It's just hard to believe you're going away," I say to Casey.

"No more fighting over the medicine cabinet," Casey says. "It's all yours."

"Right, that's priority number one," I mutter.

She sighs and gives me a look. I'm sure she's about to say something sentimental and sisterly, but instead she says, "Please stay out of my room. Don't think my stuff's up for grabs."

I blink at her and decide to follow that "if-you-don't-have-anything-nice-to-say" advice my mom used to give me as a kid. Yeah, maybe I'm not so sentimental about her leaving after all.

"We should leave at ten for the airport," Mom says. "You coming, Arielle?"

"You don't have to," Casey says.

Well, that's a relief. I dislike airports and prolonged goodbyes.

"Okay, I'll skip it, then." I get up to rinse out my bowl. "I'm going to stop by Trinkets. I need a new backpack before school starts."

"You're not going to go to the airport to say goodbye to your *sister*?" Mom says.

"It's okay," Casey cuts in. "There's not going to be much room with all my luggage, anyway."

Casey and I match blue stare to blue stare.

"Well," I say. "Say bye before you go."

"Will do," she says.

I head upstairs and get in the shower. There are empty spots everywhere in the bathroom where Casey used to have her millions of products. When I step out of the steamy bathroom, the house is dead quiet and I realize they've left already. Forget goodbyes.

I stand in Casey's doorway. She even bothered to make her bed before she left. I open a drawer: identical pairs of white underwear folded into tiny triangles. Around her mirror, sticky remnants of tape are left where she took down all her pictures. Except one. Of Casey and Perdita. It must be like five years old or something. Perdita still has braces on and brown hair. They're standing in front of a Ferris wheel. My sister is wearing a rainbow sweater that's so big, two of her could fit in it. Her arm is around Perdita, and Perdita's making a silly face, wide-mouthed and crazy-eyed. The feeling, it's like someone stuck a microscopic knife in my ribs.

"I still can't believe you're dead," I say.

It's funny how, with pictures, no matter where you stand, no matter which angle you're coming from . . . the people stare back at you.

In my room, I towel off and then notice the folded white paper on my bed. It's a note. I open it up and it says, in Casey's perfect, I-could-be-a-computer-font cursive, "Bye, little sister. Good luck in school. I'll see you at Thanksgiving." A big heart filled in with red, and then the burst of signature—*Casey*.

Now I feel bad for not going to the airport and for taking such a long shower that I even missed an in-person goodbye. I always think Casey's the cold one, that she's the reason we're not close anymore—but maybe I have more to do with it than I'd like to admit.

I put the note on my dresser top and am surprised when my breath snags into a stinging sigh.

Other than being an activities counselor at a summer camp for gifted girls last summer—which included teaching ridiculously fancy stuff that seems worlds beyond eight- to ten-year-olds, like screenwriting and calligraphy and Japanese cooking classes—the antique shop is Chloe's first job. And considering her closet is full of *Mad Men* dresses and the only DVDs she owns are black-and-white flicks from way before our time, it's a perfect place for her to work.

Trinkets and Treasures has a glittery gold-freckled sign and a huge window full of Tiffany lamps, wigged mannequins in furs, and Crayola-bright comic books. It's in downtown Velero, which is across the overpass, nearer to the airport, where rent is cheaper and burritos are better. Takes about ten minutes to ride my bike there. The bell jingles when I swing the glass door open, and right away I see Chloe there behind the register, in a flower-power-style dress and swooshed charcoal eyeliner. I stop there, in the entrance, taking in the impossibly busy surroundings. Velvet chairs and wood tables with dangling price tags, odd uniforms hanging on the walls, racks of Hawaiian shirts, and milk crates with records.

Chloe squints at an open binder and bites her lip like it's calculus. When she sees me standing in the entrance, her face brightens and she shuts the manual.

"Hey!" Chloe slips from behind the glass display cases twinkling with jewelry and watches.

We hug.

"What's up?" she asks.

"Not much," I say. "Casey just left for Cambridge."

"Aw, are you sad?"

"Kinda-sorta."

"Look at the bright side: now you can steal her clothes. Not that you'd want to."

Yeah, Casey wears cardigans and turtlenecks. I'm not exactly itching to raid her closet. "She made sure to tell me to stay out of her room."

"Of course she did."

"Anyway, I need a backpack for school. Do you guys have anything?"

"They're in the back, near the racks of coats and purses," she says. "Want me to show you?"

"I think I can figure it out."

"I believe in you," she says, fist in the air.

I laugh and head to the back.

There are a few barrels with backpacks and tote bags in them. I rifle around, but most of them are far from anything I'd wear. I pick up this old knapsack made from Mexican-blanket fabric and try to imagine myself wearing it around the halls—hilarious. That's when suddenly I get that feeling again.

It's happening, in broad daylight, in public.

I'm totally frozen, my hairs are standing on end, and I truly feel like something terrible is about to happen. I can't even move. It's awful-quiet, a storm that swells in my body. My ears ring and I get dizzy . . . and I swear something big and inhuman is standing behind me, or to the left of me.

"Hey," Chloe says.

She's peeking around a china cabinet in front of me, smiling.

"Hey!" she says again.

But she's in another world. I still can't move. She comes closer to me, her brow furrows, and she claps her hands in front of my face. It takes a second, but my ears stop ringing and I realize I've dropped the knapsack. I swallow and look behind me—where, of course, nothing evil lurks. I laugh nervously.

"What just happened?" Chloe asks.

"I spaced out; I don't know."

"You were making a sound. Do you know you were making a sound?"

I pick up the knapsack, mortified, looking in back of me again just to make sure no one saw me being a complete weirdo. "What do you mean?"

"You were whimpering. Like, 'ehhhhh.'"

I really don't know what to say. Now that I'm feeling normal again, whatever just happened a minute ago seems . . . beyond description. I giggle nervously, imagining myself whimpering.

"You're also really pale." Chloe puts her hand on my cheek. "Let's go outside, okay? Get a little air."

"Okay."

I follow her outside and we stand near the shop window in front of an old neon sign that blinks "DRINK COKE."

"I'm worried about you," she says. "You looked so far away. Are you sure you're okay?"

"I'm totally fine," I say. "Maybe I just need to drink more water."

"Has this ever happened before?" she asks.

I'm almost a little annoyed at how concerned she is. Like, making it into this big thing. I know she means well, but even a dizzy spell turns into some soap opera with Chloe.

"The other day, after you slept over," I say. "Right after you left. It happened then. I found Perdita's necklace and then spaced out and felt . . . weird. But I think I was just really tired."

Chloe's mouth drops open.

"Chloe, *stop it*. I'm totally fine."

"No, I'm just—this is so weird, because I just read this book called *The Legend of Clara Voy*. It was about a woman who was psychic."

Oh God. I prepare myself for some completely ridiculous idea from Chloe. This is the same girl who tried to convince me that she really did contact Marilyn Monroe's ghost on a Ouija board last winter. For someone so smart, sometimes Chloe can have some majorly dumb ideas.

The look on my face is obviously spelling out how skeptical I am, because Chloe feels the need to tell me, "Stop judging, okay? Stop. Seriously. It was based on a true story."

"Okay," I say, the true story thing making me a little less suspicious.

"So she had this power to read objects. It's called *psychometry*. She could pick up an object, and if something powerful had happened to someone wearing the object—usually it was jewelry—she would go into this *trance*."

She pauses dramatically.

I fold my arms. "I'm still listening."

"So she got these overwhelming *feelings* when she touched these objects. And she got better and better at it—she started seeing *visions*. And then she was able to solve murders. From just *touching* something."

"I'm not having visions; I'm not psychic; nobody has been murdered."

"All right, all right . . . but have you thought about how weird it was that it happened with Perdita's necklace?" She leans in and whispers, "Wasn't that the same night she died?"

Okay—we're in the sunshine, it's seventysomething degrees, but I just got a chill. Chloe can be super convincing. I'm a little creeped out. Still, I don't want to admit it, so I shake my head.

"I think I just need water," I say.

"There's a Starbucks around the corner, past the bookstore," Chloe says.

"I'm going to go buy something to drink."

"Come back when you're done. Seriously, this is *crazy*, Arielle. What if you're psychic?"

"Right."

I pass the bookstore and go into the Starbucks and get in line. I study the menu and all I can think about is, what if Chloe's right? What if I am psychic and I can read objects? I mean, I do believe in ghosts. Not that I understand them, or know where they are, really, but I swear I've felt them. Is it so different to think people can be psychic?

"Next," the guy behind the register says.

Oops. Spaced out there again. I grab a bottle of water and put it up on the counter. When I look up at the voice that says, "Three dollars," I can feel my eyes go wide.

Look at him: tarry, slicked-back hair. A scar above his eyebrow. Superhero biceps.

It's Raffi, Perdita's once-boyfriend.

I get a little tingle like a bug crawling up the back of my neck as yet again another person, another instance, another something has circled back to Perdita.

This town is way too small.

"Hey," I say.

"Hey," he says back, squinting his eyes at me. "Do I know you?"

"Um . . . I'm Casey's sister. Casey Delaney?"

He nods. "Ohhh."

"I think I saw you at the wake the other day," I practically whisper.

"Yeah," he says. "Sad shit."

I'm pretty sure I just ruined this guy's day. A second ago he was a happy Starbucks employee; now he slouches and stares at the register like I slugged him in the belly.

I hand him a five. "How are you?"

He shrugs, opens the register, hands me my change. "Besides the nightmares, I guess I'm okay."

I nod, relieved to know I'm not the only one suffering from bad dreams.

"It's weird to lose someone you feel like you already lost," he says. "It's like losing her again. I don't know."

I put my change in my pocket. "What do you mean?"

"She was just different, you know? We weren't together anymore so we didn't talk that much. She, like, pulled away from everybody. I don't know what was going on. I didn't think it was *that* bad, though. I mean, I let her have her space. I didn't know she would . . ." He shakes his head and lowers his voice, leans his brown arms on the counter. "I just keep thinking, *how could I have helped her*, you know? But I think everyone wonders that. Probably Casey, too."

"I'm sure," I say. "Even I've wondered that, and I didn't even know her that well."

"Everyone's acting like she was all tanked. I don't know. It wasn't her style. The whole thing, it just . . . it bugs me." He sighs. "Fucking bummer."

That seems like the understatement of the century. The door behind me opens. I turn around. An old man with a crossword puzzle book the size of a Bible stands in line behind me now.

"Anyway, tell Casey I say what's up," Raffi says in a louder, more cheerful voice that tells me the conversation is over.

"I will," I say. "Take care."

"You too."

I go outside and chug my water. As I head back to my bike, I pass the bookstore. Chloe's inside, talking to an über-tan guy with short blond hair. He's wearing a name tag so I assume he works there. She's flipping her hair over her shoulder. One of her legs kicks up behind her as she laughs at whatever he's saying.

Total flirtfest going on in there. I'm not about to ruin Chloe's game, so I get on my bike and head home. I pedal quickly, sweating in rivers as I make it up the overpass. The rivers cool me as I breeze downhill. I can see the lake from up here, the entrance once taped off with yellow and crowded with police, and eventually, I can see home.

I Google this psychometry thing and this Clara Voy person later. It does ring a little true, especially the cases I read about people who sense things *before* they happen. The woman who touched her husband's scarf, for instance, and got an itching feeling on her chest—and the next day he died of a heart attack. What if I did predict Perdita's death when I touched her necklace? But it seems so far-fetched; there's too much missing to make sense of it. It could just be a fluke.

When I go to bed that night, though, I remember something that happened right before we left for camp the summer Justin died. Justin and I were sitting at the dinner table, eating cookies and milk for dessert. And then he *froze*. His mouth dropped open, zombie-black from Oreos, and he just stared for a minute with his hand on his glass of milk. I laughed because I thought he was joking, messing around with me. But then I remember I got a little scared because he wasn't moving. I started saying his name. "*Justin? Justin?*"

He came to a minute later and do you know what he said to me? He said, "A ghost just flew out of my milk."

At the time, I cracked up, thinking he was kidding. I pictured something like Casper the Friendly Ghost, a silly cartoon.

He laughed, too, and said, "No, really! It was white and it flew out my glass . . . I felt it."

"It didn't, you liar," I said.

It was just a silly, strange moment between the two of us. We went back to eating our cookies and didn't talk about it anymore. But after he died, I thought about that moment. I don't know, it seemed to have significance somehow—that he saw a ghost—"felt" a ghost—less than a week before he himself became one.

I don't know if I believe in psychometry. But maybe I believe some people are psychic sometimes. And I for sure believe in ghosts.

Who knows, maybe the two things are more related than we think?

That night I dream that I see Perdita at a 7-Eleven-type store. She has an armful of candy, and a Slurpee in her hand. Her eyes are red and I wonder if she's stoned.

"Hey," she says. "I've never been so hungry. I just keep eating and eating—and I never get full."

I nod. I want to tell her, *you're dead; that's probably why.* But in the dream, I figure that's rude.

"Something's not right," she tells me. "I think I forgot my money. Can you spot me?"

I reach into my pocket and I pull out a piece of paper. It's got a heart on it just like the one Casey drew on the note she left me, colored in and red.

"I don't have anything," I tell Perdita.

"I'm never going to leave this place," Perdita says sadly.

The store starts crazy shaking—packaged snacks fly from the shelves, the drink cases swing open, and sodas roll onto the floor. I try to run, but it's like I'm on a ship—everything is woozy and tipping—and I end up grabbing onto shelves that fall onto me. I'm buried in food and candy.

I startle awake in my bed, sweaty and panting. I get up to pee, turn on the light, and notice that my lamp and the speakers on my bedside table are on the ground. What the . . . maybe there really *was* an earthquake? But everything else in my room seems normal. My cup of water on my dresser is fine; none of my framed pictures have fallen over. I think of ghosts, of course. I'll be sleeping with the light on for the rest of the night, thankyouverymuch.

On my way back to my room, I turn around and look at Casey's room, her door ajar. If she were here her door would be closed and her white noise machine would be whirring over her snores. It's so empty and different to see it open and hear silence. Even though we haven't been exactly best buds lately, I wonder how her first night in Massachusetts is going, if she's fast asleep, if she's lonely, if she misses us. If she's even thought of me once. I'd bet a hundred bucks she hasn't.

I hang in her doorway in the dark and listen to the nothing in there. Listen to my sister not being there. I sit on the edge of her bed and—I would never admit this to anyone, not even Chloe—I cry for a second. I can't explain why. It's just this overwhelming sadness, this void that has no name, this fear that everything changes without my asking and everything ends with nothing.

From this corner of her bed, thanks to the moonlight peeking through Casey's lace curtains, I can see the black outline of that one picture she left taped to her vanity. Just a colorless black rectangle there, the gloss of the photo catching the light. I get up and stand in Casey's doorway and shut the door behind me.

Back in bed, my eyes are heavy from the waterworks that have dried and tightened my face. I lie here for a long time, not thinking, just listening to my heart—a knocking that won't go away.

CHAPTER 5
GIRL MADE OF GLASS

THE FIRST DAY OF SCHOOL is always a total circus. No one can shut up in class and the teachers shout their syllabi. Half the school's tardy; offices are crowded with students adding or dropping classes. New haircuts and suntans and outfits distract. Some guys look better than they did in June, slimmer, more facial hair. And I swear last year's freshmen weren't this young, pipsqueaks with giant backpacks.

At lunch, Chloe and I meet up at our usual spot at the quad. A lot of people hang out here to eat on sunny days. We run into some girls we haven't seen all summer; that girl Layla with the green streak in her hair talks about riding scooters in Italy, and her friend Autumn blabs about snorkeling in Belize. Belize Belize Belize. When the bell rings and Chloe and I walk to Theater together, she says, "Well, I certainly didn't miss them one bit."

I so agree.

"You have to come over this weekend," I tell Chloe as we near the cement building and stand in front of the bulletin board rainbowed with fliers. "Save me."

"From what?"

"Mom's making me start packing for the move."

"Fun."

"Yeah."

"Well, I have plans Saturday," Chloe says. "Maybe Sunday."

"*You* have *plans?*"

Besides a shift at Trinkets, Chloe's weekends usually involve a book the size of the dictionary and/or some black-and-white movie marathon.

"Oh, I see. He doesn't happen to work at a bookstore near Trinkets, does he?" I ask, remembering how I caught a glimpse of her flirtfest through the window the other day.

She slaps my arm in surprise. "How the hell did you know that?"

"You know, telepathic powers." I put my fingers to my temples, close my eyes, and pretend to be a fortune teller.

"Really? Omigod, I was *right*—"

"Calm down. I'm kidding." I drop my hands and open my eyes. "I saw you talking to him through the window the other day."

"Whatever. You really *are* psychic," she says.

"You're psych*otic*."

"I'm going to start calling you the Great and Powerful Arielle."

"I'm going to stop calling you at all."

We giggle and go down the short flight of stairs and head inside.

It's a black box theater with maybe a hundred worn seats and a stage. The dust is everywhere in the air, dancing around underneath the yellow lights. The room's smell tickles my nose.

Pierre's our teacher's name. He doesn't have any kind of an accent, but he speaks oh-so-properly. He wears a sweater vest and rimless glasses, and is dead-serious about this acting thing.

"You are *thespians!*" he announces.

A few people snicker.

"Why does that make you laugh?" he asks.

No one answers.

I turn and scan the seats behind me to see who else is in this class, because of course Chloe sat us right in front. I hope there's no one I know. I have a feeling this semester is going to get embarrassing. I see a ton of freshmen, 'cause, you know, this is a beginning class. A couple people whose faces I recognize but whose names I don't know. I look ahead again and Pierre explains we're going to pair up and do some exercise. Chloe nudges me, like, obviously we're partners. Phew.

But then of course Pierre has to go and ruin it all by doing it based on the roll sheet instead. He calls off names, *here*s are shouted in the air, and he pairs people up. The pairs go sit onstage. When he says "Arielle Delaney" and I raise my hand, he follows it up by saying, "Texas Dell."

"Texas Dell?" he says again. No one answers.

I look around, surprised. Texas. As in *Tex*. Dell, as in, *Perdita Dell*. Her little brother, who I last saw stoned at the wake, is supposed to be my partner.

"One more time, anyone here named Texas Dell?" Pierre practically sings.

"Present," a voice says.

I turn around. Tex is in the doorway, his backpack hanging off one shoulder and a motorcycle helmet in hand. He's apparently just arrived, ten minutes after the bell. He looks different than the last time I saw him, and it's not just because he's wearing a jean jacket instead of the wrinkled shirt he was in at the wake. He's gotten a haircut and shaved.

"Next time you're late I'm marking you tardy," Pierre says with a frown.

"Yes, sir," Tex says, almost sarcastically.

"Please have a seat, Texas."

"Please call me Tex," Tex says, as if he's imitating him.

Some girl in the back row giggles.

"Tex. Okay." Pierre makes a notation in his black book. "You'll be paired up with Arielle. The two of you, join the others onstage."

I stand up and Tex looks at me. His eyes widen like *whoa* and he gives me a nod, puts his backpack down, and the two of us walk up the wooden stairs onto the footprint-dirty stage. We sit cross-legged. I stare at his profile out of the corner of my eye as Pierre pairs up everyone else. A warm sadness spills along with the memory of Perdita and the wake. The way she looked in the coffin, so unlike herself. Her brother's nose and eye-shape are replicas of her nose and eye-shape. I try to imagine what he must be feeling, but that's all I can do—imagine. It must be so different losing a sibling when you're his age rather than when you're barely even old enough to read.

Sometimes I wish that I could vacuum other people's pain away, that I wasn't so powerless, that I could do more than just stand by and watch how wrong the world can be.

Arielle, a voice in my head says, stop being such a downer. Focus. Pierre is talking. Also, Chloe's paired up with this tiny freshman who won't stop looking at her boobs, and that's enough to make me smile again.

"The face," Pierre says, pacing the stage around us pairs, "is a window to the soul. Acting is too often *misconstrued* as performance. Good performers are good observers."

This guy seems to be the king of catch phrases.

"We're going to start off by sitting opposite our partners, legs crossed," Pierre goes on.

We do. Now Tex's turquoise gaze is on me. We're so close right now that I can see he's wearing an A-line tank beneath his tight white T, I can see his Adam's apple quiver. Our knees touch.

"Gaze into each other's eyes," says Pierre. "Be comfortable. Look right into their eyes. Don't giggle; don't shift. Remain completely still."

This sounds easy, but it is absolutely painful. It takes every ounce of willpower for me to keep staring at Tex's face. I have to think about something else, like who he reminds me of, other than Perdita of course. Someone on TV. Is it James Franco?

Pierre's shoes squeak as he paces around us, watching us staring, frozen, into each other's eyes. He's probably getting a real kick out of this. Teachers can make students do such idiotic things. Someone giggles and Pierre says, "*Silence*," and the giggling stops. What is Tex thinking about me? If I had realized someone was going to be studying me this closely I would have worn more than mascara this morning. Some foundation so you can't see the zits on my nose wouldn't hurt. I would have sprayed the flyaways down on my hair.

I hear Chloe clear her throat. I would know Chloe's throat-clearing anywhere.

"You must feel absolute control over your face, over your *mask*," says Pierre (he pronounces it like "mosque"—now he apparently thinks he's British). "Try to observe each individual part of your partner's face, *feel* it in your own."

Must I?

Sigh. Fine.

I start with Tex's eyebrows. He must pluck them. Those brows are way too shapely for a guy. I move on to his nose. What can I say? No complaints there. Hello, lips. He's definitely wearing Chapstick. Moving on. Amazing what being clean-shaven will do for a face. He looks so much better than when he had that scruff on his cheeks at the funeral. And again it's kind of hard not to see the resemblance to Perdita. The shapes of their eyes especially, the sleepy slant. It's almost like she's still alive there, in his features.

Clearly, the Dells are a beautiful family.

"Now," Pierre's heels click closer behind me. "Try to say 'I love you' with an eyebrow, or an upper lip."

Oh, geez. This is so dumb. Please. I can't stand the tension, so I do this Elvis-thing with my upper lip where I raise one side and open my eyes super silly-wide. Tex's eyes flash and I can tell he's fighting a smile. Now I'm fighting a smile, too. It feels good to make someone happy, even for a split second.

"That's wonderful," Pierre says, leaning down. "Wonderful job." His heels click away.

Tex smiles big (and if we're counting details here, he's definitely had braces at some point and uses some kind of teeth whitener) and I smile big back, relieved, the nervous tension dissolving. Then his face goes deadpan again.

Pierre orders everyone to lie down with our feet opposite our partners', our heels and toes matched up and pressed together.

"Press your feet together. *Feel* their energy. Experiment with moving your legs together as if cycling." Pierre claps. "Become one body. Cycle slow, slow now, that's right. Now change it up! Cycle fast!"

Seriously? This should be illegal. This is the stupidest thing I've ever had to do in a class, and that includes the day in Health last year when Chloe and I did a rap about anorexia nervosa.

Whirring sounds fill the air. Speak of the devil, there's Chloe next to me, her shiny hair splayed on the stage floor.

"I hate you for making me sign up for this class," I whisper.

She pretends to not hear me, cycling faster.

Finally, Pierre tells us it's done. We sit up. Some girls fix their hair some boys groan.

"In the theater, when a scene is done in rehearsal, we simply say 'Scene,'" Pierre says. "And, speaking of scenes, when I call your name, please come up and get a copy of the script I have prepared for you and your partner, written by the great master of the theater, William Shakespeare."

When Pierre gets to my name, I come over and he hands me two packets. "A scene from *Much Ado about Nothing*."

I walk across the stage and give a copy to Tex, noticing his sideburns for the first time. Okay, Arielle. Exercise is over. You can stop studying him now.

"*Much Ado about Nothing*," he reads. "Looks like a lot of words for a bunch of nothing."

"Yeah," I say.

"I almost didn't come today," he says. "I almost dropped out and tried to crash Woodshop instead."

"Well, then you wouldn't have gotten to stare at my face like this for twenty minutes," I say, widening my eyes and staring at him, frozen.

He laughs. "Yeah, that was weird."

"I still don't get the point," I say.

"At least I got to stare at you and not that guy." He points at an overweight, zit-pocked guy across the stage. "I guess I should consider myself lucky."

I smile. "Yeah, could have been worse."

"Hey . . . thanks for being so nice," he says.

At first I'm taken aback—what? How am I being nice? But then he finishes his sentence.

"At the wake," he says. And sadness passes over his face, like a shadow.

"Oh," I say, my smile dissolving. "Don't thank me."

"You were the only one who just *talked* to me. Didn't try to walk on eggshells or give me advice. I really appreciated it. It was a . . . little glimmer in an otherwise horrible day."

"Sure," I say. "I told you, you can talk to me anytime. I mean it."

We stare for a moment. It's like the whole loud room, the squeaking shoes and papers shuffling and Shakespeare being read out loud . . . it all disappears, and it's just me and Tex, sharing a moment that is so deep and heart-prickling I'm not even sure where or who I am for a minute.

But then the bell rings and I'm just Arielle again, in fifth period. And he goes back to his jean jacket and his motorcycle helmet and I go back to my tote bag and cardigan.

"I'm Ophelia!" Chloe squeals as we leave class.

"Who's that?"

"Hamlet's girlfriend. She loses it and drowns herself. I'm so excited!"

Tex passes us and waves bye to me with the rolled-up script. Chloe puts her hand over her mouth as he passes.

"Oops," she says once he's out of earshot. "God, I hope he didn't hear that part about drowning herself."

I turn around and watch him turning a corner, swinging the motorcycle helmet.

"I don't think he heard," I say.

"He cleaned up nicely, didn't he?" She glares at me playfully. "I can't wait to talk about everything later."

"Me, too. That class was ridiculous."

The second bell rings. We're late, so we spring in opposite directions, I to Trig and she to Pre-Calc.

Chloe isn't waiting for me near the bus like she said she would be after sixth period. I'm almost worried about her until I squint and see her in a red car with bookstore guy near the pickup loop. Damn. They seem to be moving fast. I don't even know his name and I'm her best friend. I text her: *Thanks for offering me a ride, traitor!!* And follow it up with a winky face, just to let her know I'm not *that* mad.

The bus blows with a capital B. How many screaming, deodorant-deficient freshmen can you cram in one place? Is it even legal? I haven't taken the bus in forever because Casey used to give me rides home. I can barely move in this seat. As some guy's backpack hits my face, I miss my sister bad, for selfish reasons. Also, I should get my license. I always think that, but this time I mean it; I really should.

I have to push my way through the disgusting bus to get off at my stop. I'm sweating. I need a shower after that bus ride. I walk briskly toward my house. Across the street I can see clear to the other side of the lake. I pass houses and try not to think about Perdita's as I near it. But I can't help it. It's a magnet for my eyeballs as soon as it comes into sight: the bleached-gray two-story house that freezes me in place. I stop cold and stare at it, right here in front of me, drink it in. The downstairs windows with parted curtains, the glimpse of a piano inside, the hanging plants on the patio, the open garage with the motorcycle's silver parts catching the sunlight. I stare at the house like I expect it to grow legs and its windows to blink, as if it's something alive and not just a house.

I know which upstairs room is Perdita's. I know because our house is actually laid out identical to theirs, except in reverse. A mirror image. Lots of houses in our neighborhood are the same design, cut from the same giant cookie cutter. In their house, Perdita's room is where mine is. She told me that before, peeking in to say hi when she was over.

"Hello, weird version of my room," she'd say before heading to Casey's room.

Yes, the sun is shining in my eyes, nearly blinding me even though I'm wearing shades. But for a second, out of the corner of my eye, I swear—no exaggeration—I see a flicker of platinum hair in her window. A blink of a blond ghost. In the window that, were it my house in a mirror, would be mine. She looks right at me and raises a hand in the air, slowly, an unwaving wave. And then she shuts the curtains.

I'm stunned.

The curtains are drawn. Black curtains. The only dark curtains of the house. That couldn't have just happened. Right? My imagination is seriously a disease. But it was undeniable. She stood there with screaming-blond hair and waved at me. I watched her close the curtains. I saw, and there's just no way to argue that I didn't.

Ghosts. In the daytime. My heart is all *bam-bam-bam*, fireworks inside my chest. I'm getting overblown with creepy-crawly goosebumps in the sunshine.

And then, as I stand dumbstruck looking up at her night-black window, the front door swings open. Tex steps across the lawn and into the garage. He doesn't see me standing here on the corner of his lawn like a weirdo, thankfully. He's got a wrench in hand and squats, squinting at the motorcycle. It takes about a half-second for me to strut up the sidewalk (not too fast; don't want to be too obvious) and pretend I haven't been standing like a creeper, gawking at his house. I look up the street and tell my pulse to shut up as if the outside world can hear it.

But as I glance back over my shoulder, in that half-second, he looks straight at me. And even as I turn back ahead and walk away acting faux-normal, I can feel him watching me. Burning a hole in my back.

"Arielle?" he yells.

I turn around and wave.

He stands up with the wrench in his hand, covering his eyes to block out the sun.

"See you tomorrow," he yells.

"Yeah!" I say, maybe a little too chipper. "See ya."

Cool. He didn't seem to think I was weird to just be standing in front of his house with a staring problem. His gaze lingers on me like he wants to say more. I wait a second and then turn around and keep walking.

I'm almost past the house next door now when a head pops over a rosebush out of seemingly nowhere and spooks me, so crazy I let out a little mousy squeak.

"Friend of Perdita's?"

I stop and put a hand to my chest, calming myself. I'm so jumpy! Why the guilt, brain?

The owner of the voice is a man, staring back at me, over the rosebush, through the rosebush—there are rosebushes surrounding his whole front lawn like a freaking botanical garden—and he's wearing a floppy pink gardening hat that is totally a lady's hat. Not that there's anything wrong with that. But, you know, kind of a surprise. He's also sporting pink gardening gloves too small for him and wielding a spade. His eyes are blue and buggy; his bald head is enormous; his skin sags like putty.

That's when I realize that while I've been standing here analyzing how totally gross he looks, this man has been waiting for me to answer his question.

"Umm . . . no," I say, because I don't have the time or energy to explain the complicated and twice-removed relationship I had with Perdita. I smile politely and wave. "Bye."

"Bye," he says softly, an almost flirty smile turning up his lips. I feel his eyes on me as I walk up the sidewalk and . . . it's not like when Tex's eyes were on me, a moment ago; it's a stare I wish would stop. One, two, three . . . STOP ALREADY.

I'm not usually quick to judge, but I'm not into the way he looks at me. He's grandpa-aged. I'm sixteen. But I pretend he doesn't exist, and he's just a weird old man in a woman's hat complimenting me. I head home, quickening my pace this time. Who cares about that man?

I wish I could backpedal about twenty or so feet for one more glimpse of the Dells'. I want to look back. Not only to triple-check the window and make sure I didn't just see a ghost . . . but to linger in that moment with Tex and his shiny motorcycle, and that stare he gave me. Like "bye" wasn't enough. Like he was looking for the words to keep me there. Like he could see what was inside me at that moment. Like I was a girl made of glass.

CHAPTER 6
TO SEE THE MORNING

S ATURDAY I COME DOWNSTAIRS for breakfast, pour myself a bowl of cereal, and grab the paper to read my horoscope, then I just about choke on my Cheerios. On the front page, at the bottom, there's a black-and-white picture of Perdita— her senior picture, looks like—and a headline that reads, "TOXICOLOGY REPORT IN ON VELERO DROWNING VICTIM."

I scan the article with hungry eyes and a palpitating heart.

Toxicology results show eighteen-year-old Perdita Dell who drowned weeks ago at Lake Los Caballos, didn't have drugs or alcohol in her system.

A preliminary autopsy report confirms she died of asphyxiation although her cause of death is still under investigation. The final autopsy report will be available in October.

Anyone with information on the case is urged to contact Velero PD.

I turn the page. I can't believe that's it, that's the whole article. My stomach turns and I put my spoon down on the table. So she wasn't on drugs and she wasn't drunk. So . . . how did she drown? And what does that mean, her death is "still under investigation"? I don't understand.

I pour my cereal down the sink and flip on the garbage disposal. I get dressed in my room, where my mom has stacked some flattened boxes as if to say, *hey, get packing already.* A little over two weeks until I have to say goodbye to my room. Plus, I'm supposed to have my lines for my *Much Ado about Nothing* scene for Theater memorized by Monday and I can barely remember my character's name. And my partner didn't even show up to class the last two days, so I didn't get to rehearse. Knowing my luck, Tex probably dropped out and took Woodshop after all, and I'll have to perform the scene with Pierre. Kill me, please.

I wish I could go back to bed and hide from the world.

Saturday's gorgeous, but I don't leave the house or my pajamas. Instead I zone out on bad TV and procrastinate on homework and packing. When I go downstairs for a snack, Mom is packing up books and has a bandanna tied to her head like Rosie the Riveter, which means she's not messing around today. She only busts that thing out for spring cleaning and getting ready for garage sales. Dad has made a big "to chuck" pile in the middle of the living room to give to the thrift store.

I'm so not ready for this.

"Did you see the paper today?" I ask.

They both stare at me like they have no idea what I'm talking about.

"The article about Perdita on the front page?" I ask.

"Yes, very sad," Dad says flatly, as if his mind is elsewhere.

"A bit surprising," Mom says, squinting at a book in her hand. "I assumed drugs played a part."

"You're still not dressed?" Dad asks with a glance and two raised eyebrows. As if someone in a Muppets shirt and saggy sweatpants should judge.

"I hope you're packing up there," Mom says, giving me The Look. You know, the Get Your Crap Together look.

"I still have a couple weeks," I say.

"What are you *doing* up there?" she asks. "It's three in the afternoon."

"Memorizing my lines for Theater," I lie.

"I'm getting a little tired of your laziness," Dad says.

"So*rry*," I mutter, and go back to my room.

When Chloe calls at five, I'm sure she's going to rescue me from my boredom. But instead she tells me she can't help me pack because she's going on a date tonight with The Guy Who Has No Name. And tomorrow she works all day.

"Who is this dude?" I ask, annoyed. "I just know him as Bookstore Guy."

"Oh, his name is Brody," she says. "You'll meet him soon, I'm sure."

"So, are you guys, like, a *thing* now?"

"Yeah, we're seeing each other."

Dead silence on the line. I know I should be happy for Chloe—I don't want to be selfish. But this has kind of blindsided me. She's always been über-picky and shy about guys—she hasn't had an official boyfriend since she dated that guy Grayson (yes, his name was Grayson, and he wore sweater vests) on the debate team at the end of ninth grade. And now overnight she has some boyfriend who doesn't even go to our school.

"How old is he?" I ask.

"Not that old. He's nineteen. He's a freshman at City College."

She's kind of gushing. Gross.

"Where are you going on your date?" I ask.

I feel a little pinch of envy on that last word there. Honestly? I want to go on a date. I want a guy to take me out. The closest thing I ever had to a date with Conrad—stupid Conrad, with a head filled with nothing but penis jokes and sports statistics, who had the nerve to dump *me* right before finals—was when I went over to his house and we sat on the couch watching basketball on TV. He made me a frozen dinner once. Does that count?

"Some sushi restaurant. And then we're going to the gym."

The *what*? Chloe won't even ride a bike because she hates exercise so much. Her only worry on her report card is her PE grade every semester.

"How romantic," I say.

"Shut up. He has a guest pass. I went with him on Friday afternoon, too. We did a spinning class together and I tried the weight machines. I am soooo sore."

The thought actually crosses my mind that I'm dreaming. But no. This is too drab; must be real life.

"Well, have fun," is the only nice thing I can think to say.

I thought Saturday was a bummer, but Sunday promises to be even worse. Mom and Dad are somehow in grouchier moods today. They're both in the garage. There's a pile of junk in the middle of the cement floor—which I see includes my pink bike with the streamers from when I was a kid. I stand in the doorway between the kitchen and the garage, a granola bar in my hand.

"You're not getting rid of my bike, are you?" I ask.

"Oh, look who decided to get up," Dad says. "Is it noon yet?"

It actually is noon. Not that he has to be such a jerk about it, though. I'm a little surprised, because Dad's usually a total softie and a goofball. But he has that wrinkle in the middle of his forehead that tells me today is a good day to steer clear of him. It happens.

"Yes, we are getting rid of your bike," Mom says.

"But I rode that thing for years." I remember all the summers riding it to and from the lake, the park, the nearby elementary school. It was my first bike without training wheels.

"Well, you're too big for it now and someone else could use it," Dad says.

"Can't we keep it so I can, like, give it to my daughter one day?" I ask.

"There's no storage at our new place," Mom says, chucking a bunch of Christmas lights in the pile. "We're getting rid of a lot of stuff."

"The Christmas lights?" I ask in disbelief. "We use those every year."

"We're moving into an apartment," Dad says. "There's no need for them. And here's an idea—if you have so much to say about what we keep and don't keep, why don't you actually pitch in and help out?"

He sounds so mean and un-Dad-like, my nose burns like I might cry. Mom throws a Santa decoration in the pile.

"I'll start packing my room today," I say quietly. "I just . . . I didn't know it was an apartment we were moving into."

They don't say anything. I go upstairs and close the door. I stare at my white walls, stunned, imagining leaving this house I've been in my whole life. For an *apartment*. No back yard. No Christmas lights. For the first time it becomes real—we're actually leaving. In weeks. I hate the reality of it.

After trying on some eyeliner and doing my hair three different ways for no reason, I finally assemble a box and start packing. I start with my closet, sweaters I haven't worn in forever and shoes I forgot even existed. I try to cheer myself up by watching some *Phantom Animals: True Confessions* while I put things into boxes, but without Chloe here, it just seems cheesy and stupid. After I've assembled the second box, I get a knock on my door. I know it's Mom because her knock always goes *knock-knock* and Dad's is just one loud *KNOCK*.

"Yeah?" I say.

She opens the door. She has her cell in her hand and she's holding it out to me.

"Casey wants to say hi," she says.

"Oh, okay, thanks."

She closes the door. I stare at the phone for a sec before putting it up to my ear. I can't believe Casey's been gone for weeks already and this is the first time I've talked to her.

"Hey," I say.

"Hey, Arielle," she says. "How's it going?"

"It's okay," I say. "Actually, it's lame. I'm packing my room."

"Getting ready for the move."

"Yeah." I sit on my bed. "How are you?"

"I'm doing well, actually," she says, almost like she's surprised to say it.

"Have you started classes yet?"

"Yeah, I have. So far so good."

"Are they super hard?"

"Well, I haven't turned in my first papers or taken any tests yet, so we'll see," she says. "But they're fascinating. It's not like I'm taking English, Math, and Spanish. The classes are really specialized and there are so many interesting ones to choose from—I'm taking a seminar on Buddhism and ethics and an African music history class."

She sounds so happy and light compared to the flatline she was when she left. I almost can't believe it's been such a short time.

"That sounds cool," I say. "What are the dorms like?"

"Nice," she says. "The people I've met so far are friendly. My roommate is this girl from New York named Savannah. She's a violinist and she's pretty amazing. We're a perfect match for living together."

"Why, is she a total neat freak?"

"Yes," she says. "And she's an early riser. And she's just really sweet. I feel like we were instantly friends."

"Does Emily live in the dorms with you?"

"Um, no. I actually haven't seen much of Emily since I got here," she says. "She lives in a different building and we don't have classes together. This place is huge. I mean, it's like a small city." She's quiet for a second. "But I'm blabbing all about me. What about you?"

I wrack my brain for something interesting to tell her, but compared to dorming with violinists and taking classes on Buddhism, Velero High seems like a pretty dull place.

"I'm okay," I say. "It's been a boring weekend. And I already hate school and it's only September."

"I'm sorry," she says.

It's so weird, how nice Casey is being. Is this what happens when your sister, AKA the biggest pain in your butt, moves a coast away? Suddenly she becomes nice and actually listens to you again?

"Also, Mom and Dad are being assholes," I say. "They're so stressed about the move, I don't even want to go downstairs."

"Well . . . you do know what today is, right?"

"Sunday?"

"Arielle, today is Justin's birthday," she says. "You know how they get on his birthday."

I suck in air and close my eyes. "I totally forgot."

"Yeah. That's part of the reason I called today. Not that I brought it up, of course, but . . . I know today is hard for them."

I stare at my unmade bed, the sadness suddenly here, entering and filling my room like an uninvited guest.

"He would have been twenty-two," Casey says.

"Hard to believe," I say.

"Yeah." She sighs. "So cut them some slack."

"I will," I say. "I feel like such an ass for not remembering."

"It's okay," she says.

There's a pause big enough to swallow me on the line. I think of so many things at once—pictures of Justin's birthday parties (I remember pictures more than the real thing, since I was so young when he died); the candles my parents always light for him on the night of his birthday; the impossible him that would have been twenty-two. What would he have grown up to become? What would he have looked like? He would be old enough to drink now, old enough to graduate college. It seems like trying to imagine a fictional character, a myth.

"So light a candle with them tonight," she says.

"I will," I say. "Hey . . . did Mom tell you about the news article about Perdita?"

The silence is so long I wonder if the phone dropped the call.

"Hello?"

"No, she didn't," Casey says. "Why, what did it say?"

"She wasn't on drugs or drinking when she died, that's all."

"Yeah, I knew that. I've talked to the police a couple times since I've been here," she says.

"Really?"

"Well, yeah. They're still investigating what happened to her." Her voice gets smaller and she sounds more like the Casey who left Velero—tired, monotone—not the Casey who has been electrified by Harvard. "Now they're making it sound like maybe it's suicide. I think they're just grasping at straws at this point."

"Why would it have been suicide?" I ask, surprised. "Did she leave a note?"

"No." She exhales loudly. "They think because she deleted her Facebook account and quit school suddenly that, I don't know, it could have been on purpose."

"What do you think?"

"I honestly don't know and I don't even know why it matters at this point," Casey says. "She's dead. I'm heartbroken about it. But speculating as to whether it was an accident or suicide, it just seems pointless. I wish the police would stop calling me. They already interviewed me before I left town and I told them everything I know."

"I didn't know they interviewed you."

"Yeah. Anyway, I should get going," Casey says. "I have to finish this paper for my Shakespeare class."

"Hey, I have to memorize a Shakespeare scene for Theater."

"Really? I didn't know you were taking Theater. I can't believe I've never thought of that before. It's perfect for you—a natural drama queen."

She says it like she's delivering a compliment, but I frown, annoyed. Oh yeah, now I remember why I found her so obnoxious before she left for Cambridge.

"We'll talk soon," she says.

"Talk soon," I echo.

"Wait—one more thing. Will you help Mom and Dad pack my room for me? I would have done it myself before I left but I ran out of time with all the craziness that happened."

"Sure," I say.

"Don't touch anything; just put it in boxes exactly the way it is," she says.

After we say goodbye and hang up, I decide that, yes, my sister is officially the Most Annoying Human in the World again.

That night, after we order pizza and clean our plates, my parents and I each light votive candles at the table and wish my dead brother a happy birthday. My mom wipes away tears and my Dad sobs a few times, but otherwise we sit pretty much in silence. I'll be honest with you: the whole thing is depressing, and we do it every year. It makes me uncomfortable, the quiet, the sadness that's too big to even talk about, the candles flickering and the prickly-neck, goosebump-skin feelings making me wonder if Justin is here and if he cares whether or not we remember his birthday. But I do it for my parents. This year, it's worse because Casey isn't even here. It feels lonelier and smaller and sadder than ever. I don't know what the "right" way is to celebrate someone's birthday who's dead. Cake? Presents? Obviously the normal stuff won't do. But this ritual of ours always feels so the opposite of celebratory, sometimes I wish we'd give it up. Even thinking it, though, makes me feel like the worst sister ever.

"We love you, buddy," Dad says as he blows out the candles.

That night, it takes me a while to fall asleep. I'm bothered. I don't know if it's the move coming up that bugs me most, or if it's Chloe and her boyfriend with the stupid name and her new gym-going ways, or if it's bigger than that—thinking of Perdita committing suicide by throwing herself into the lake, thinking of the man my brother will never be—but I'm anxious and afraid in my own room, so much so that I get up and turn on the light in my closet because I'm not in the mood to see ghosts tonight.

But I see them anyway.

I have this dream. In the dream I'm at school, in the quad where Chloe and I usually eat lunch, only it's empty. It's so empty it's almost apocalyptic—there's trash on the ground, the buildings are decrepit and weather-worn, and the grass has grown tall in the planters and engulfed the flowers that once were there.

I'm really scared, for some reason, like I know something bad has happened here, or is going to happen, and I'm not sure where to go. That's when I feel someone's arms slip beneath mine from behind me. Someone wet and cold is trying to pick me up. I turn around and scream "NO!" And I see it's Perdita. She's dripping; her hair is hanging in strings; she's pale blue and wearing the cheetah-print dress she wore the day I saw her body being pulled from Lake Los Caballos.

"Come on," she says. "Justin's party's starting."

She tries to tug my arm.

"I don't want to go!" I tell her.

"It's just right there," she says, nodding toward the cafeteria. The double doors to the cafeteria are open but the place looks desolate and dark and people-less.

"Don't you want to see him?" she asks, pulling my sleeve.

I start running away, toward the theater building, down the cement stairs, and that's when I wake up kicking and whimpering in my bed. I sit up, shaking, and I've never been so glad to see the morning.

CHAPTER 7
BETWEEN SLEEP AND WAKEFULNESS

The next day, at lunch at the usual spot in the quad, I don't tell Chloe about my crappy weekend, the sad memorial for my brother, or the ghosts that visited me in dreams last night. Not because I don't *want* to tell her—I just can't get a word in because she's gushing the whole time about Brody. I've only seen the guy through a window. I know I don't really know him. But already I don't love how every conversation these past few days is all about him. Plus he sounds like a weirdo. He loves spinning classes. He gave her a juicer and convinced her to give up solid foods. And today, instead of reading a battered fat paperback, she's flipping through a glossy magazine with a blond, tan chick on the front called *Bod*. It's open to an article called "Fab Abs in 10 Minutes a Day."

I feel miles away from her.

Truth be told, I feel miles away from everyone today. Look at the crews on the bleachers. The skinny Colgate-smile cheerleaders giggling and pointing as they drink their smoothies.

Autumn and Layla, loud-voiced and neon-haired on a bench next to us, blabbing about whether Beemers are better than Benzes. Couples making out like they're not surrounded by a hundred other people. So many worlds. None of these people looks like the type to have nightmares about dead people, or worry about moving into an apartment, or wonder, late at night, alone under their sheets, if they see ghosts.

Nope, that's just me. And I can't even talk to Chloe about it. I sit here picking at a piece of pizza while Chloe drinks slime in a jar and pores over her magazine. I don't even know what to say right now. I've been chewing this bite of pepperoni for minutes.

"It's really good," she says, swirling the sludge around in her jar. "Try it! There's half a head of kale in here."

She has a green juice-mustache over her lip.

"No thanks," I say.

"I had hot lemon water for breakfast with cayenne," she says. "Cleans out the colon. Veggie juice for lunch; fruit juice for an afternoon snack."

"That doesn't seem healthy," I say.

"*That* doesn't seem healthy," Chloe says, pointing at my pizza. "So much grease and carbs."

The silence is long and uncomfortable, which is, like, unheard of. Chloe and I don't *have* awkward silences. It's part of the benefit of BFF-dom. So I aim to fill it.

"Has Brody brainwashed you?" I ask.

I say it jokingly but she sees through me and gets offended, rolls her eyes.

"No, of course not. I'm just on a health kick."

"What about chocolate?" I ask.

Chloe is a chocoholic. We can't go to the mall without her making a beeline for See's. She has a T-shirt she wears to bed that says *Will run for chocolate.* You can always trust her to have a candy bar in her bag.

"I'm cutting out sugar," she says. "Just to retrain my palate."

She might as well have just told me she is going to run off and join the Marines. I have to will my jaw to not drop.

"Are you doing this to lose weight?" I ask. "Because you're not fat."

"No!"

"Are you doing this for Brody?"

"No! I'm just trying to be healthy. Can't I try to improve my lifestyle for my own reasons?"

"Of course," I say.

Although it's kind of a coincidence, isn't it, that you suddenly want to change your lifestyle the same week you start dating a health freak, I don't say.

"It's just . . . weird," I say carefully. "Exercising, juicing, cutting out sugar . . . it's not like you."

"People are allowed to change, Arielle," she says, offended.

She says it at the exact moment the bell rings. Everyone around us starts cleaning up their trash and picking up their backpacks and going to class. Chloe stuffs her *Bod* magazine back into her bookbag and gulps the rest of her slime.

I want to say something more, something like, but do they *have* to change? Do you, of all people, have to throw me a curveball when, seriously, I've had enough already in the last couple of months to last until adulthood and beyond? But I just stand up and throw my pizza crust in the trash. We grab our bags and head toward Theater and I bite my tongue until it hurts.

In Theater, there's a post-lunch excitement that buzzes in the room. Pierre has to do a lot of clapping and *shhh*-ing people. Also, remember, there are a ton of freshmen in this class and let's face it: freshmen are the loudest, most obnoxious humans on earth. We have to pair up with our partners and go find somewhere to practice our scenes. And I guess I have a little ounce of luck today, because Tex shows up (tardy, of course), and that means I don't have to rehearse with Pierre again, whose breath smells like rotten coffee and who says the lines so loud that my ears hurt.

"It's a nice day," Tex says, coming over with his script rolled up. His shirt, a blue-green T with a wolf on it, perfectly matches his eyes. "How about we go outside?"

"Sure," I say.

It is a nice day. Such a nice day my kinda grumpy self almost resents it. Like, day, do you have to be so nice? Excuse me, sun, do you have to shine so very much when I feel like a little storm cloud inside? Tex and I step out the door and walk to a nearby tree, where we plop in the shade and open our scripts.

He studies it hard, his dark brow furrowing, and takes a deep breath. But before he dives into the lines, I interrupt him.

"Where were you the last couple days?" I ask, pulling a yellow-headed dandelion out of the grass.

"Oh," he says, and looks up at me. "I don't know."

It seems like the weirdest response to a very simple question. I laugh. "You don't know where you were?"

He rests his chin on his fist, his elbow on his knee. "I just didn't feel like coming."

"Well, I hope you keep showing up," I say.

He watches me. Actually, I can tell he's watching my lips. Why on earth would he want to? I didn't even wear gloss today.

"Why?" he asks. "'Cause you care about me?"

He says it sarcastically, delivers it like a little verbal slap.

"Actually, no, for selfish reasons," I tell him. "I have to rehearse with Pierre when you don't show up. He has major halitosis."

He smiles into his hand. "Gross."

"Yeah, do you know how awkward it is having to say 'I love you' to your teacher?"

"Like it's that much better saying it to me," he says, tearing a small clump of grass.

"Actually, it's about a thousand times better," I say.

He rains the grass down in the air. "Should I be flattered?"

"Sure, be anything you want," I say. "Just . . . don't ditch class anymore."

"You don't like weed; you don't like ditching class." He brushes off his hands and looks at me. "You're no fun."

"The school year just started," I say. "Seriously. You don't want to end up getting suspended by midterms."

If you ditch a certain amount of classes, and it's not even that many, school suspends you. I've had warnings myself, and I haven't even skipped that many.

"I don't really care," he says. "It's not the first time I've been suspended."

He looks me in the eyes. His eyes are painfully bright, and I notice, for the first time, his stupid-amazing lashes. Why do guys always get the to-die-for lashes? Such injustice.

"What's wrong?" I ask softly. Even though I'm pretty sure I know the answer. I remember the newspaper article, and what my sister said on the phone the other day about suicide. I wonder how his family took the news.

He plucks a dandelion from the ground. "You'd be better off asking me what's right."

"Okay." I stare at my script, the pink highlighted lines. "It's cool. You don't have to talk about . . . whatever's going on."

"I'm fine." He crunches the dandelion stem between his fingers, rubbing back and forth until the stem flattens and squishes. "Let's just do the stupid scene."

"I'm not an idiot," I say. "I can tell you're not fine. I'm the queen of not fine. So I should know."

He looks up at me. "What does *that* mean—you're the queen of not fine?"

The words and feelings pile up in my mouth. I'm almost angry with him for not caring about class, for thinking I can't understand pain, when I am in a terrible mood after a crappy weekend and have plenty to worry about myself. I tell myself, Arielle, shut up. Just shut up and read your lines and don't tell this boy about what's inside you.

But like usual, I don't listen to me.

"Did you know my brother drowned?" I ask.

He sits up straight and his eyes widen like I've suddenly come into focus.

"Are you kidding?" he asks.

"Yeah, I thought it would be really funny to joke about that," I say sarcastically.

My hands are shaking. I have to hold them together to make them stop.

"My brother drowned at summer camp," I tell him. "It was . . . let's see. Ten summers ago. But I still remember it like it just happened."

"You were *there?*" he asks, leaning in.

I nod. "I watched them pull him from the water. The counselor tried to do mouth-to-mouth—yeah, I was there. I saw everything. He died right in front of me. I was six."

"Holy shit," Tex says.

"This weekend was his birthday." I have to close my eyes for a second to stop my burning eyes. I open them again and look up at the tree above us, its emerald applause of leaves, as if I expect to see Justin's ghost there. Then I look back at Tex, who is watching me like a movie that has him on the edge of his seat. "My parents were total assholes all weekend long and I couldn't figure out why. Then I remembered—oh yeah. My dead brother. He would have been twenty-two."

He puts his hand on my hand for a second, and I'm shocked by its warmth. After a second, he pulls it away.

"I'm sorry," Tex says. "I didn't know about all that."

"You don't need to apologize," I say. "I guess I'm telling you this because I want you to know that I do understand. I really do."

I want to tell him more. I want to tell him I saw his sister's body, too. Maybe I even want to tell him I have nightmares and think about ghosts way more than a healthy teenage girl should. But I stop there. I've already said too much, considering how little I know the guy.

We just stare, and the warm breeze washes over us, and we keep staring.

And once again, this stranger—or this twice-removed somebody—this boy I hardly know enough to deserve to be exchanging such a lengthy look with—turns me into the Girl Made of Glass. And the heat I feel isn't just from the sun up there. No. It's all through me. It's heat from the inside.

"I like your hair today," he says. "All wild."

"I didn't do anything to it."

"Maybe you should not do anything to it more often."

I smile, touch my hair to make sure he's talking about *that* wavy uncombed mop.

"Are you going to make a wish or what?" I ask.

He looks down at the dandelion between his fingers, at the ashy head, hundreds of wispy seeds ready to be blown, waiting for their beginning in a new patch of earth.

Maybe change isn't always bad. Without change, there'd be no beginnings.

He inhales. I think, good luck, seedlings. I hope you land someplace lovely.

He exhales and the dandelion head disappears, and the seeds soar away, away, away, in all directions, a hopeful cloud.

"So," I say. "What was your wish?"

He chucks the stem across the lawn. "No way I'm telling you."

"Fine, I don't want to know your stupid wish anyway," I laugh.

"I'd tell you," he says, staring at me, hard. "But I really want this one to come true."

My heartbeat slows in my chest. And I notice, for the first time, the parts of his face that are his own and not his sister's. His cheekbones. The olive complexion. His bottom lip.

I'm on the Internet that night, looking up ghosts. What a recipe for more nightmares, Googling ghosts right before bed. But I'm just curious if other people see ghosts in dreams, feel ghosts in their room, the way I do. The answer, which comforts me, is yes, a lot of people think they can communicate with ghosts. So many people, in fact, that my four words typed innocently into the search box—"Do you see ghosts"—have generated thirty-five million results. The first result is an article called "Eight things to do if you see a ghost."

1. "DON'T FREAK OUT." Okay, thanks for that advice, dude, but . . . when you think there's a ghost in the room with you it's kinda hard not to get spooked.

2. "TRY TO COMMUNICATE." Been there, done that. I would be embarrassed to count how many times I've talked to who I thought was Justin while alone in the room. Did he ever talk back? No.

3. "TAKE PICTURES." Sorry, but when I think there's a ghost near me, it happens so fast—and is so paralyzing— the thought to grab my phone and start clicking away doesn't even come to mind.

4. "RECORD SOME AUDIO." See number three. While you're at it, see number two.

5. "CALL OTHERS IN." I can just imagine how my mom would react if I called her into my room because I swear I saw a ghost . . . back to the therapist's couch I would go.

6. "WAIT IT OUT." As opposed to . . . ? Of course I wait it out. I mean, what else is there to do?

7. "DOCUMENT IT." Like, basically keep a diary of your ghost sightings. This actually could be a possibility, although I can't even bring myself to do most of my homework, so who knows how consistent I would be about documenting ghost sightings.

8. "RETURN." As in, return to wherever it was you saw the ghost. Considering I've seen them in my own room and my own house, this is kind of a no-brainer.

"This is stupid," I say, closing my laptop and sitting up on the bed.

And bam.

The feeling rolls in first—I'm heavy, my ears ring, and everything's suddenly wrong, like the room itself is sick.

Then I see it.

Oh no.

I'm not kidding; to my left—*I see her again.*

The skeleton girl reappears like a blurry negative of a photograph. Her hair is white, she's got holes for eyes, and she's still as a photo. She doesn't move. She repeats across once, twice, and then faster, faster, fasterfasterfaster across the left side of my room, infinitely. Like wallpaper.

She's superimposed over my walls and ceiling; when I open my eyes wider, she's all over my furniture and my clothes on the floor. And as moments pass, she begins to morph. Her colors brighten. And she fills in, more human with every blink—flesh paints her cheeks peach; her eyes emerge in those holes and appear human. It's like I'm watching an identical army of someone decomposing in reverse, and there she is, unmistakable. I even see a heart ticking there, neon red, beneath her dark jacket. Then her replicas, her paper doll–like ghosts, disappear in an instant.

"Perdita?" I whisper, my pulse gong-loud and conga-fast.

My hands tremble. I swallow and swallow. It's more than a sign—it's real, she's here with me—I mean, I was just reading about ghosts and then there she was. From skeleton to unmistakable girl-I-knew. Filling the room.

I'm so scared she'll reappear that I get under my sheets and turn toward the wall, ball up, and squeeze my eyes shut. I put a pillow over my head.

"Go away," I whisper. "Just go away."

I don't let my eyes open again, even though I'm dying to check behind me to see if she's there again. I imagine the skeleton girl lingering above me, behind me. And even though it's ridiculous, I just keep repeating the words in my mind, *protect me, Justin. Protect your sister.* I repeat them until they become a mantra. And finally—how, when, who freaking knows—I slip away into a blissful, dreamless sleep.

When I wake up the next morning, the first thing I do is sit up and stare at the corner where I saw the skeleton girl the night before. Now, in the light, it seems silly and I wonder if maybe I was nightmaring again.

It's strange how, these days, I'm having trouble telling the difference between sleep and wakefulness.

CHAPTER 8
THIS WORLD BEHIND

The day has finally come. I protested. I procrastinated. And yes, more than a few times, I cried. But today there's a moving van sitting in front of the house, and bearded, buff guys in white shirts are running in and out of the front door with cardboard boxes, lamps, furniture. My room is nothing but traced shapes on the carpet, the phantom of where my bed was hours ago, lines of dust where my dresser sat for years. The carpet remembers what the space has already forgotten.

I can't believe we're moving.

I know we're moving less than two miles away. I should swallow it and shrug and say whatever. But as Mom pulls up into the parking spot of the apartment that's apparently my home now, I'm filled with something new. Not a good new, not pretty shivers. It's a new I don't want, a change I'd rather reject. It's an *apartment building*. There are college kids smoking cigarettes on a balcony and kids splashing in the pool. I mean . . .

talk about a step down. Although, actually, we're on the third floor. Two flights of stairs. Apartment 3G.

"It's really not that bad. I think you're being a drama queen," says Chloe, who should know, being *the* drama queen herself. She has dropped weight in just the couple weeks since she started "juicing" and "eating Paleo." Her dresses, which used to hug her curves, have loosened. Not only that, she has taken to spraying herself with fake tanning spray and looks . . . orange. I blame Brody for everything, and I've still never even met the guy. But to be honest, at this moment, Chloe's tangerine skin tone and diet are hardly the hugest deals. I've got bigger changes bugging me for the time being.

We're standing in my new room stacked with boxes. It's probably three-quarters the size of my last room, and instead of looking out onto a quiet street and the eucalyptuses that line Lake Los Caballos, its view is of a parking lot filled with cars.

I hate it.

"The closet's huge," she says, popping the light on and stepping inside. "I mean, seriously. You could sleep in here."

"Why would I want to sleep in a closet?" I say.

She pops the light off. "God, grumpy much?"

"Come on, you have to admit this place sucks."

"I mean, it's smaller. But it's got its charms. The huge windows are a plus."

"So I can better see the gross parking lot?"

She stares at me with charcoaled eyes. "Okay, did I come here to listen to you whine about the inevitable or to help you unpack?"

"Help me unpack," I mutter.

"Okay, so hand me a box and let's get started."

We start putting clothes into my dresser.

"You're too skinny," I say.

She rolls her eyes. "Don't start on that again."

"You just look different."

"I'm *healthy*. I'm *exercising*."

She's also more irritable without carbs and sugar, just a little something I've observed.

"You're not eating enough," I tell her.

She gives me a sidelong look. "Geez, you are worse than my mother."

I refold a sweatshirt on the bed. "Has *she* met the infamous Brody?"

"Not yet."

"I'm a little offended you haven't introduced him to your BFF."

"I will! God, what is this, rag-on-Chloe hour?"

"Sorry," I say. "I'm just in a bad mood."

"Aw," she says, rubbing my arm. "I know you're bummed about the move. Try to think of the positives. Namely, that we can walk to each other's houses now in less than ten minutes."

"Yeah," I say.

There are other positives. For one, I don't have to stare out at the lake every day and think about the terrible day Perdita's body was discovered. Also, I'm ninety-five percent sure that house was haunted. Maybe I'll leave my creepy skeleton-girl sightings behind.

There's one loud KNOCK on my door. That means it's Dad.

"Come in," I say.

He has a bag of store-bought cookies in one hand and his phone in the other.

"Cookies?" he asks.

There are crumbs in his beard, but I decide there's no point in telling him.

"No thanks," I say. "I ate just a little bit ago."

"Cookies?" he asks Chloe.

"That's okay," she says, waving her hand.

"Wow—are you sure you're feeling okay?" he asks Chloe.

"I'm eating Paleo," she tells him.

My dad nods for a long time, which I know means he has no idea what the meaning of Paleo is.

"You look tan," Dad tells her. "Did you go somewhere?"

"She went to the drugstore and bought a spray," I say.

Chloe whacks my arm. "Shut up."

"It's true!" I say. "She has a new boyfriend."

"Ohhh," Dad says. "I see. Are you guys going steady?"

We stare at him, not knowing what the hell to say, until Chloe bursts out laughing.

"What does that even *mean*?" she asks.

"Dad, you can go now," I say. "You're embarrassing."

"Aw, I'm embarrassing you?" he asks, pinching my cheek and talking in a baby voice.

"No, you're embarrassing yourself," I say.

"Touché," he says in an oh-so-proper tone. "Hey, when are *you* going to get a boyfriend, Arielle?"

"Her partner in Theater is looking pretty promising," Chloe says with a coy smile.

"What? Shut *up*!" I almost yell.

"Oooh, tell me the deets," Dad says. He shoves a cookie in his mouth.

We stare at him again.

"Dad, seriously, you can go," I tell him.

He holds up the phone. "I was about to call Casey—you want to say hi?"

"Not now," I say, gesturing to the disaster that is my new room.

"Ah, okay. I'll give her your love."

"Thanks."

"'K. Peace out, bras." He closes the door.

Chloe smiles and sits on the bed. "Your dad is the biggest dork."

"Duh."

"Now I know where you get it," she says.

"Whatever, I'm not a dork like him. It skips a generation." I put my hands on my hips. "Um, and excuse me, what the hell was that? Acting like I'm into Tex?"

"Oh, come on, I see the way you guys are in class with your intimate little conversations."

"We're friends," I say.

"You convinced him to stop ditching—obviously he likes you, Arielle."

"It's not like that," I say, frowning. "Our sisters were best friends. We just—we understand each other."

"Okay, use whatever euphemism you want," she says, smiling.

I'm not into being teased right now.

"God, stop getting all butt-hurt," she says. "I'm happy for you is all. Plus, he's hot. You could do a lot worse. Cough-Conrad-cough."

"Hey! Conrad wasn't that bad."

"Yeah, but he was no James Franco doppelganger, either."

I'm quiet for a minute. It has crossed my mind lately that Tex likes me a little bit. I mean, he started coming to class every day and told me it was for me. He smiles more when we're alone together, rehearsing. It also has crossed my mind that he looks a little bit like a teenage James Franco sometimes. But I don't know. It's too weird.

"I overheard you rehearsing. You guys had some chemistry in your little *Much Ado about Nothing* scene," she says.

"It's called acting," I tell her. "Okay, stop staring at me like that."

"You're blushing!"

"It's hot in here," I say, opening the window. "Seriously, it's getting dark. Let's finish unpacking, please?"

"Okay, okay."

While I finish putting my jeans in my dresser, Chloe rips open a big box on the floor.

"Board games!" she says.

"Oh, that's from the living room," I say. "They must have put it in here by mistake."

"OMG, it's been years since I played Candy Land." She leans down and starts digging through the games. Then she gasps. "Arielle! Can we *please* take a break? Please? I want to play with this."

She pulls out a long, red, beaten-up box. I haven't seen it in what seems like years, but I recognize it right away. The Ouija board.

"Please?" she whines. "Remember how last time I talked to Marilyn?"

"Oh, come on."

"Just for a few minutes!" she says. "We've been unpacking for hours. I gave up my day off with Brody to help you."

Right. She could have been on a romantic date at a spinning class or making a salad. I forgot what a sacrifice she made to be here today.

"Fine," I say, rolling my eyes.

"Do you have any candles?" Chloe asks.

"Really, do we have to be all cheesy about it?"

"There is nothing cheesy about ambience," she says.

I sigh and dig through my top dresser drawer, where I remember I packed my little Cheshire Cat candleholder in a sock. I pull it out and light the votive candle inside with a lighter. Chloe turns off the light and plows a bunch of my clothes into a corner to make room on the carpet. She sets up the Ouija board and I sit across from her, putting the candle between us on the floor.

Honestly, I've never been a fan of Ouija boards. I'm too spooked about ghosts to love them. But with Chloe, she's always so focused on contacting dead celebrities, it never gets too heavy.

We put our fingers on the heart-shaped plastic.

"Okay," Chloe says solemnly. "Let's be quiet for a moment and invite the spirits to speak to us."

I actually, privately, silently, ask the spirits to *not* speak with us. Hey spirits, I say in my head, how about you don't come here into my new room and scare the living crap out of me like my last room? But I'm not really that scared. Ouija boards are made by Parker Brothers and sold at Walmart, for crying out loud.

My candle flickers on the floor.

"Is anyone here who would like to speak to us?" Chloe asks.

Slowly, beneath our fingers, the plastic pointer moves to "YES." I don't like it, but I know it's Chloe doing it, so I'm not actually freaked out or anything. We'll probably just have a short discussion with Audrey Hepburn or something in a minute and then be on our merry way.

"Who are you?" whispers Chloe, staring at the board with wide, concentrating eyes.

The plastic pointer slowly coasts over all the letters, circling, and then lands on the "P."

That's when my stomach flips and I feel gross. My pulse quickens and I want to take my fingers off, but the pointer keeps moving. It circles around and then settles on the "E."

Perdita.

I take my fingers off, stand up, and flip on the light.

"I don't want to do this," I say. "It's a waste of time."

"Come *on*," Chloe says.

"I need to unpack," I say.

I would prefer to vomit, actually. I'm breathing like I just ran a marathon. I'm overwhelmed by this idea that the ghosts that were in my last room are just as present here, in my new room. I can feel it. I can imagine the skeleton girl right there, to the left of my bed, just the way she was before.

"You are no fun," Chloe says. "Seriously."

She stands up and sighs. I can't believe she doesn't get it— that she doesn't even flinch at what "P-E" spells. For someone who's practically a genius, Chloe can be pretty slow.

"Were you really scared?" she teases me.

"No," I say. "I just think it's dumb."

We empty boxes. She helps me make my bed. I turn on music to fill the silence. When we're done, the room resembles my other room, only it's like the walls all crawled in a foot or two. It's arranged the same, with the bed beneath the window.

Chloe hugs me when she's ready to go. Apparently Brody and she are going to go to his place to do some late-night Pilates. Gag me.

But as she reaches for the door, she gasps and turns around.

"Oh my God," she says, her hand over her mouth. "I just realized: *P-E*."

I wait for her to say her name. Say the name of the girl who's been haunting me for months now, Chloe, just say it.

But instead she says, "Peter Sellers. I just watched *Dr. Strangelove* last night! *Peter Sellers*."

"Probably," I say.

"'Night," she says. "Enjoy your new room."

"'Night," I say. "Enjoy your yoga-and-granola date."

She sticks her tongue out at me as she leaves. A few months ago, she'd sleep over, no question. This time I didn't even bother asking her. It's weird how when we hang out, I can tell she's itching to be with Brody. Texting him, checking her phone, always only partly here.

Maybe it's not just homes and rooms I've exchanged. My whole world seems to be crawling toward something different, and who knows? Soon all of it, all my nouns—people, places, and things—could be unrecognizable.

The first night in my new room is weird. I have trouble falling asleep. I can hear my parents' voices through the wall now—they used to be so far away in the old house. What if I hear my parents boning or something? Do my parents even bone anymore? God, this whole move has filled my head with totally yucky thoughts.

I'm relieved that I don't see any ghosts in my new room. But I lie awake for a small forever, thinking about the Ouija board and how I didn't like the way it spelled out "P-E" without me wanting it to. Why won't these dead people leave me alone, leave my head so I can move on? I'm starting to feel just a little bit crazy.

Another unsavory thought enters my mind in the dark as I stare at my new cottage-cheese ceiling. I remember, again, how just days before Justin died, he saw the ghost fly out of his glass of milk. It sounds so weird, but then again, I've seen some pretty weird things now myself. And I wonder for the first time if seeing ghosts could be a warning. Like, a warning from a world beyond that you're in danger, that you're going to die.

What if these are more than just simple ghost sightings—because really, why would Perdita haunt *me* when she could haunt my sister, or her own family? No, maybe it's deeper than that. Maybe ghosts come to those who are soon going to cross over.

No, my bones cry. But I don't want to die!

This thought flashes over me like an instant flu and I sit upright in my bed, gasping a little, and run to the switch to throw on the light. My hands are shaking. The Ouija board is sitting on top of the box of games, still, and I take it and run to our new kitchen and cram it in the garbage.

"Arielle?" Mom asks.

She's sitting on the couch in the living room, watching me with a glass of wine in her hand. It's so dim—just a soft lamp beside her—that I didn't realize anyone was up.

"What are you . . . doing?" she asks.

"I don't want this anymore," I say.

"Want *what*?"

"The Ouija board," I say.

She peers at me through her reading glasses in total confusion.

"Okay," she says finally. "Are you . . . feeling okay?"

"I'm fine," I say. "Goodnight."

"'Night," she says in a voice that still says *you're crazy*.

I go back to my room and leave my door cracked. I lie in bed and listen to the sounds of people in the parking lot. The dumpster opening and closing. Car doors thumping, footsteps clacking, someone laughing on a balcony. Even though my room is arranged the same, it's unfamiliar; I'm a stranger in my own home, and I can't see a future for myself. I just see blankness. And for the first time, I'm not afraid of ghosts coming to visit me, or of the reality that they exist—I'm afraid of being one. Of leaving this world behind.

CHAPTER 9
OCEAN FLOOR DEEPER

I'T'S OCTOBER ALREADY. Every Halloween I swear I'm going
to devise some marvelous costume, and then October thirty-
first sneaks up—oops—and I go running to the sales rack at the
drugstore for some super-lame, on-sale costume-in-a-package
nobody wants, or I fall back on my good old cat ears and cat tail
yet again (done that one five years and counting, thankyouverymuch). But that's not going to happen this year; no ma'am. After
school today, I walk to Trinkets on my way home from school
(it's in my neighborhood now, a benefit of the new place, I
guess). Costume-hunting enables me to procrastinate just a little
more on my homework, which is always welcome. Plus, I might
think up some ideas for an amazing, original costume and get to
say hi to Chloe, who ditched lunch all week to go make out with
Brody in his car (gag). Autumn's having a Halloween party this
year and she's supposedly inviting half the school. So. I want to
find something killer.

I go into Trinkets, the bell-on-the-door jingling, and am disappointed to see the old woman with the crooked lipstick instead of Chloe behind the counter. Also, the "Halloween section" is one garment rack with outfits that are mostly shoulder-padded, sequined numbers fit for a flamboyant grandma. I actually contemplate, for about half a second, being a grandma for Halloween. No, Arielle. Just no. I stand for a long pause, remembering the feeling I had last time I was in here—the spooky chill, the paralysis I usually only get in the privacy of my room when I think I'm being visited by ghosts. And I look at these souvenirs lining the walls and shelves, all of them once having belonged to someone else. Morbid, I know, but an antique store suddenly reminds me of a shiny, colorful graveyard, and I get a feeling like invisible fingers brushing across my neck as I think it.

When I leave the shop, I look back in the window for just a glance—and I swear a little blond doll in a rocking chair blinks her black-lashed eyelids.

My freaking imagination.

Through the window of the bookstore next door, guess who I see? It's the king of spinning classes and juicing, himself. He's on the phone behind the counter. I have no real reason to go in there, but I've *still* yet to meet the elusive Brody. I just want a closer glimpse of the guy my best friend is so obsessed with she won't even eat lunch with me anymore—or eat lunch *period*, for that matter.

So I push the glass door open and step inside.

He doesn't even look up at me. Brody is blond, with a curly mop of hair, tan as a surfer. He's wearing a button-up shirt with a name tag pinned to it, and his arms are buff. I try not to stare like a creep, though, and head straight for a rack of books that says "PARANORMAL" behind him. While I stare at the book spines—they have everything from the hunt for Bigfoot to

UFOs—I eavesdrop on his one-sided conversation and decide he must be talking to Chloe.

"Do it," he says. "I'm ordering you." He laughs. "Yeah, but I've always been a blond guy. It won't hurt, I promise." Pause. "You are such a baby." Pause. "Do you care about my opinion or not? I don't understand why you called me to whine about this if you don't even care what I think." Pause. "Just do it, you already bought it. I told you I want you to." Pause. "I love you too, baby." Pause. "I *do* think you're pretty . . . doesn't mean you couldn't be prettier." He laughs.

Even though his voice sounds nice, playful, as if every sentence he utters is half-joking . . . Brody sounds like a total A-hole. I can't believe someone as deep and smart as Chloe would fall for *him*.

I get distracted from the conversation, though, because my eyes fall on a book called *Real Documented Ghosts*. I pick it off the shelf and flip through the pages, an icy feeling oozing up my arms. It's almost like I'm repelled and don't want to look, but my hands and eyes have other ideas.

Some of the pictures are old, in black and white, of simple round lights in graveyards or long mysterious trails on staircases. Some of them have blurred faces in the background that appear almost like double-exposures. But these were taken in the days before Photoshop, right? So they have to be real. Some just resemble smoke, or vapors. There's one frightening picture of a little girl's face in an upstairs window, and my ears ring as I remember I saw Perdita up there in *her* window the day I strolled by their house. And then I get to a picture called "Specter of Newby Church" and, for a brief moment, I forget how to breathe.

The colorless, pixelated photograph is of what looks like a church organ with a fat cross on it, and a rail, or maybe a simple altar, extending in front of it. The stained-glass windows are out of focus in the background. There are three stairs below the altar. And on the right-hand side, at the bottom of the stairs, is a tall, transparent figure in a black cloak with a stretched, noseless face and holes for eyes. It's absolutely terrifying. And it reminds me so much of the skeleton girl—seriously, just put some hair on it and lose the cloak and that's *her*—that my ears start ringing and my whole body stiffens and freezes up. As I keep staring, it happens again, just like it did in my room that one night.

The skeleton on the page begins to change.

It flips from black-and-white to color. Eyes appear. Blond hair oozes from the naked skull. Lips bloom in the mouth area, reddening in a flash, and the black cloak shifts into the shape of a leather jacket. Beneath the jacket, the glow of a blazing, beating heart echoes one word in synch with my mind: *Perdita. Perdita. Perdita.* It isn't until I close the book and my eyes for a minute that I can breathe again.

Really, very, super-duper scary.

I open the book again, this time to the intro. I scan the part about how all the pictures are authentic, blah-blah-blah, and stop at this part.

Why do some people see ghosts, while others don't? It's a frequently asked question in the paranormal world. Simply put, some people are more gifted or spiritually in tune than others. They just seem to have a natural "window" into the other world that is sealed off for most other people. For others, people from beyond might be trying to communicate with them for a reason, such as ghosts whose gruesome deaths were unresolved or unsolved, or ghosts found in haunted houses who might be trying to relay a story from their past, or who may just refuse to leave a space. It is common for people near death to see ghosts. Numerous nurses and chaplains have reported this phenomenon. People on their deathbeds have commented on seeing spirits around them and have even had verbal exchanges with them. There is no cut-and-dried explanation for this, but many believe that, when close to death, the other world opens up to the living who are soon to cross over.

Okay. I am fully, a hundred percent creeped-the-hell-out now, and I have to stop reading this. I'm thinking of Justin and the ghost that flew out of his milk. I'm thinking of *me*—and this is the part that sickens my stomach like I ate something rotten. The thought that I've pushed from my mind returns. What if all the ghosts I've seen lately mean *I'm* going to cross over to the other side?

I leave the bookstore without even giving Brody a glance. After what I just read, the thought of Brody and Chloe just seems petty and dumb. I'm scared for my life.

As I hurry out the door and to the corner where the crosswalk is, I almost run into a guy and have to back up and mumble an apology. That's when I look up and realize I know him. It's Raffi. He's holding his Starbucks apron and standing at the bus stop. He squints at me with black-brown eyes.

"Hey." He points at me as if he's trying place me. "Casey's sister?"

"Yeah, sorry," I say.

He laughs. "You okay? You look like you just saw a ghost."

Whoa. I utter about the fakest-sounding laugh ever. "I'm fine, just . . . in my own world, I guess."

"How's Casey?" he asks.

"Good, enjoying college life," I say. "You?"

"I'm better," he says. "Still sad about everything, you know, obviously, but, like, moving on as much as I can."

"Cool," I say, nodding. I squeeze my backpack straps. As nice as Raffi seems, I'm anxious to get home, distracted by the thought of that picture—I can't shake the Specter of Newby Church. "Well—"

"Hey, has she mentioned the cops to you?" he asks in a low voice, stepping closer. "I mean, did Casey talk to the cops? Because they've been questioning me . . . it's been weird. I'm not sure—are they questioning everyone?"

"I think they are," I say. "They've talked to her a few times. You saw how that report came back and showed Perdita wasn't on drugs, right?"

"Right, well, I knew that already," Raffi says. "Perdita didn't do drugs."

"Casey said the cops maybe think it was suicide," I say.

He nods. "That's what it seemed like, the questions they were asking about the Facebook stuff and everything."

I scrunch my forehead, confused. "You mean—how she deleted her account?" I vaguely remember Casey mentioning that.

"Well, yeah, but *why* she deleted her account. The crazy posts and shit."

The confusion on my face must be obvious, because he starts talking slowly, as if he's breaking it down for a five-year-old.

"What that guy was saying about her, harassing her— threatening her. Posting those creepy pictures on her wall of corpses and shit."

"I don't know about any of that," I say. "Casey didn't say anything about it."

"Sorry, I'm just blabbing." He steps back and looks embarrassed. "I just wondered if you knew anything."

"I don't," I say. "But . . . who knows? They're still investigating."

"Yeah," he says.

The bus comes along, chugging like a mechanical beast and spitting open its doors. Raffi waves at me and gets on, and I cross at the crosswalk after it leaves.

Head to toe, on my short walk home, I'm bothered. I'm bothered by those pictures of ghosts, I'm bothered by what I read, and I'm bothered to think someone would bother Perdita like that. As I leave the avenue with restaurants and shops and duck onto the quieter streets with maples and apartment buildings, I think about that report a girl in English presented last year, about how cyberbullying leads to suicide. It's so sad to think that Perdita might have been suffering so badly and no one had any idea. And then again, the thought of someone posting pictures of corpses on her wall—yikes. Does that cross a line into something else? What's the difference between bullying and threatening your life?

For the first time, I let the thought come to mind: what if it wasn't an accident *or* a suicide?

But no, I think, panting as I hurry up the two sets of stairs to apartment 3G. I can't let my imagination spin out of control. I have better things to worry about right now—like me.

I try to forget the image of the Specter of Newby Church and the memory of the skeleton girl. I laugh at myself in the mirror as I brush my teeth before bed, saying, "You're not going to die, you dumbass." I watch some not-even-funny comedy show with a laugh track, to distract myself until I fall asleep. I don't see ghosts, and I don't dream of them, either. Phew. But when I wake up in the morning to the sound of my clock radio, my night table beside my bed is on the ground, toppled over; my speakers are strewn across the room; and my black lamp is broken, the ceramic body cracked, the lampshade warped.

You'd think we were rattled by an 8.0 by the looks of it. Or burglarized. But everything else in my room looks fine—just my night table was pushed over with what looks like violent force. My head hurts as I stare at it, and I cover my mouth with my hand. All I can think is, crazy as it sounds, a ghost must have done it. The night table is exactly to the left of me—the same side the skeleton girl appeared on both times. I don't know if there's a connection, but I blame her. And I sit there, staring at the mess, wondering *why*—why would a ghost be haunting me? Even following me to my new apartment? Justin's been dead for ten years. I know it's not him. But I can't help but think of Perdita, that for some reason she's the one doing this to me. Remember what that book said yesterday, about people being haunted by ghosts whose deaths were "unresolved or unsolved"? Maybe Perdita is trying to tell me something—although why *me* is beyond understanding, and I have no idea how breaking my lamp would help anything. Or it could be I'm going to cross over . . .

"No," I say out loud. I get up and straighten my night table back to its standing position, return my speakers to their places, bend my lampshade back into symmetry. I put the lamp back on the table. Cracked, bent beyond repair—it looks pathetic. "I'm going to be fine."

I get ready for school. For once, I'm actually *relieved* to be heading to the world of boring assignments and fifty-minute-period allotments of time—because at least there are no ghosts there.

Chloe doesn't show up to lunch, as usual, and doesn't even come to Theater. I text her; nothing. Maybe she's sick? But today's the day we're doing our final Shakespeare scenes, and I can't believe that even the worst flu would keep her away from the most important graded assignment of the semester thus far. I sit next to Tex in the back row as we watch everyone perform their scenes. I'll be honest: most of them make no sense to me because, as everyone knows, Shakespeare is basically a foreign language. The only one that's halfway clear is Romeo and Juliet because who hasn't heard *that* clichéd love scene before?

Tex and I climb up onstage when Pierre calls our names. We hit our marks on the floor, where Pierre told us to be when he blocked us. And, besides one part right in the beginning, I never say "line"—I remember everything. With my memory, it's truly a miracle. Pierre laughs a bunch, like he's the only one getting the jokes, which I guess he is. Tex is a good actor, which makes it easier for me to pretend like I'm a good actor, too. And when Beatrice and Benedick confess their love (the awkwardest part of the scene), we squeeze our hands together and get our faces close the way Pierre told us to in rehearsal. I can smell the fruity gum Tex is chewing. Damn, I should have chewed gum. I probably have dragon breath right now. Tex winks at me as if to say, *Relax. It'll be over soon.* And it is. Soon everyone claps and we get off stage and Pierre is singing our praises—literally, he sings them.

"Wunderbar!" he belts out like an opera singer. "Very well done, you two."

After rehearsing that damned scene for over a month, I can't believe it's over. Poof, done. It's actually kind of anticlimactic. Tex and I take our seats. He smiles at me and, between our seats, he squeezes my hand again, like he did in the scene— only we're not on stage anymore. It gives me a warm shiver that starts in my fingertips and ends in my lips, and we stare for so long I have to finally look away. He pulls his hand from mine and shoves it into his pocket. Pierre calls for Chloe and her partner, Toby, next—I can't believe Chloe missed her scene! But then I hear her voice.

"I'm here." Chloe steps out of the dark doorway, where she has apparently been lurking with her backpack in the shadows. She must have slipped in late during my scene and was afraid to sit down. But . . . that isn't Chloe. No way—I'm looking at the wrong person. This girl is platinum movie-star blond.

My mouth opens wide.

"Oh! You changed your hair color," Pierre says. "And . . . you're tardy."

"Sorry," she says, with a pained smile.

This is one for the history books. Chloe is *never* tardy. Not to mention the shock I cannot shake at her hair. From this distance, across the room, she looks like your typical California girl—fake-tan and bottle-blond. I hardly recognize her. As she climbs onstage with Toby (who Chloe and I call "Boobface" because he's always staring at her boobs instead of her face), I remember that one-sided conversation I overheard with Brody. It was him. *He* convinced her to do this to herself.

I think it might be possible to hate someone you've never even officially met.

"She looks . . . different," Tex whispers.

"Yyyeah," I say.

Tex stares at her as she finds her mark onstage. He's probably like most guys, thinking blond + tan = hot. Guys are so freaking typical. All they want are Barbie dolls.

"No offense," Tex says quietly. "But she looked way better before."

I give him a sidelong glance, surprised.

"I don't know. I'm just not into girls who look fake."

"Really? You're the minority. I feel like most guys want that," I whisper.

"No." He turns to me, almost fighting a smile. "I want the real thing."

He turns back to the front and we watch the scene. I can feel my blood ticking in my wrists, and I let myself wonder, fully, for the first time, if Tex likes me—and if I might like him back. That's crazy. I've known him so long, and our sisters and their history . . . but there's something about the way our gazes lock sometimes, and the vague somethings he says, that make me think it's not totally insane. I think of the smell of his gum and what his mouth would taste like.

Okay, enough, Arielle. Chloe's onstage now and you're getting seriously carried away.

I expect Chloe to be fabulous in her scene—she is the natural actress, and the one who signed us up for the class in the first place. She knows just where to pause to be extra-dramatic, and her voice quivers with emotion. Except, she has to yell "line" at least six times before the scene is halfway over. And Boobface is a horrible Hamlet, which is not helping matters. His voice is squeaky and high. I still can't believe she did that to her hair, but I'm trying to move past it. She keeps combing her bangs with her fingers as Boobface struggles to remember *his* lines. When she finally ends the scene with her "woe is me" bit, she really seems to mean it. Pierre doesn't say anything when their scene is done; he just makes a little notation on his clipboard.

"Yikes," whispers Tex.

I'm really surprised to see her bomb like that. I mean, I can't remember one time when I ever outshone Chloe—it's truly upside down.

When the bell rings, Chloe zooms out of class. What the hell? She doesn't even stop for a word with her best friend after pouring peroxide on her head? I'm offended. Tex and I walk out into the hall together. He swings his motorcycle helmet.

"I'm a little bummed," he says, staring at his Vans. "That it's over."

I have no idea what he's talking about until he looks up and clarifies.

"The scene," he says, pushing the hair that falls into his eyes behind his ears. "I don't know . . . it gave me an excuse to talk to you every day."

Flattery pricks me from head to toe. I'm tempted to check behind me—are you sure it's not some other girl you're staring at like that? Me? *Arielle*? The girl with holes in the knees of her jeans who often forgets to brush her hair in the morning?

The hall bustles—kids rush to classes, yell, someone bounces a basketball—but every sound seems to shrink, every movement blurs, and I get tunnel vision. It's just me and him, here. This world is small and ours.

"There's a Halloween party," I tell him. "At this girl Autumn's house. Chloe and I are going. You should come with, if you're not busy."

"I'll go, sure, yeah," he says.

"I'm glad you seem to be feeling better," I tell him.

"Shit still sucks," he says. "But . . . I don't know. I feel like I have things to look forward to again."

The bell rings.

"Crap," I say.

"I won't make you late," he says.

"'K, see you!" I yell, running to Trig.

Zoning out in Trig, I want to be mad about Chloe and her sudden Brody-inspired makeover and the fact she's been mostly MIA these past few weeks. But instead, I'm just amazed about the whole exchange with Tex today. I knew we had a connection—I've tried to be super nice to him since Perdita, and I opened up to him about Justin—but it runs deeper than that.

Like ocean-floor deeper.

CHAPTER 10
I HAD A TIME MACHINE

CHLOE AND I have always been totally anti when it comes to slutty Halloween costumes. The world needs another fishnet-legged French maid or hiked-skirted she-devil? Please. So when my ride comes (blond Chloe sitting shotgun and Brody, the infamous *Brody*, driving), I'm a little shocked. Not just because I'm being introduced to Brody as I climb in the back seat and lie through my teeth, "Nice to meet you," pretending I haven't already spied on him through a window and over a store bookshelf. But because Chloe's wearing a mermaid costume with nothing but plastic shells covering her boobs— and Chloe still has some serious C-cup boobs, even though she's lost enough pounds that her collarbones are obvious. Still, Brody feels the need to squeeze her "love handles" and tease her to "suck it in" within two minutes of me getting in the car.

Brody also loses immediate points for listening to Sting. Who is he, my mom?

"How's it goin'?" Brody says in the most bored voice known to man. Brody's idea of a Halloween costume is apparently a bunch of blood spattered all over a white T-shirt.

"Sorry we're late," Chloe says.

"It's cool," I say.

There's something oddly icy in the air—not the air conditioning, I mean, but the lack of conversation, the way Chloe stares out the window and Brody grips the steering wheel—that makes me wonder what the tension's all about. As we drive to Tex's, I can't help but gawk at Chloe's nearly bare-naked torso in the side mirror. How can she have the guts to wear such a scanty costume to the party? Every guy around is going to drool over her, possibly even Tex. The thought of which makes me sad. I look down at my boring black shirt that shows no cleavage whatsoever and wonder if I maybe should have tried a little harder to look attractive.

Brody is now singing off-key along with the radio about Roxanne putting on her red light. At the top of Chloe's head, tiny black roots are growing in. We pull into Tex's driveway and instead of letting me text him or run out to ring the doorbell, Brody gives a few quick honks.

As we wait, I notice, to the right, over the hedges in Tex's neighbor's yard, the guy with the lady's gardening hat standing on his porch with arms akimbo, staring at our car. I don't know what's creepier—that guy, or the window ahead and up above, where I swore I saw Perdita's ghost that one day. I don't let my eyes linger on it, remembering that spooky-ass photo of the little girl's ghost in the window from that book. Not now, goosebumps.

Tex comes out of his front door and jogs up to the car. He's dressed normal, jean jacket and black jeans, but he's got zombie makeup on. Black lips. White-green face, shadows under his eyes. He climbs into the back seat with me and smiles, and I'm a bit mesmerized. You wouldn't expect zombie makeup to make a guy more attractive, but somehow it's kinda hot.

"You look great," I say. "Wow."

"So do you," he says softly.

I see Chloe studying us in the rearview with a nosy stare as we pull away from the Dells' driveway. Brody turns up the song and Tex and I grin at each other. He pats my hand and I get an electric tingle that moves quickly up, up, to my chest.

After a zip on the highway, a turn up the hill, a few windy roads, Brody's SUV pulls into the long driveway of Autumn's huge Spanish-style house lined with low palm trees. It's the end of twilight; the stars are beginning to pop out and shimmer. The town below sparkles with dot-sized lights and an ocean behind it—ooh la la. The music is already bumping from inside. Tex and I jump out of the car and slam our doors, but Chloe and Brody don't. The car's still running. Chloe and Brody immediately start talking to each other, but I can't hear it through the window.

I knock on Chloe's window. She rolls it down. "We'll be in in a minute," she tells me.

"Just *go* if you want to go—" Brody says to her.

"No, I'm not going unless you're going," Chloe says.

"It's a high school party," Brody says, sighing. "This shit is embarrassing."

Chloe looks back at me and rolls her eyes. "We'll be in soon, okay?"

"Sure," I say.

Tex and I walk toward the front door, which is decorated with black and orange balloons and bowls of candy large enough to feed a small chocolate-loving country. Back in the SUV, Chloe talks in an animated way—by which I mean she's possibly yelling—in the front seat of the car. Geez. Real great relationship those two seem to have, there. I move on, into the party, where the music thumps and the lights are low and the kids drink and dance.

Autumn's dad is a TV producer or something, so her house is something out of a magazine. Wall-sized windows, sleek black furniture, chandeliers. I've been to Autumn's before, but it's never really struck me how over-the-top this place is. I mean, it's basically a mansion, and Autumn lives here with two parents who are rarely ever even home. What a waste of space, right?

The stereo system booms invisibly with techno that seems to be coming from everywhere. Twenty or so people slouch around in costumes drinking out of plastic red cups. Robin Hood. A dead bride. Autumn's a slutty devil (surprise, surprise). Superman on crutches chats up a stewardess near the snack table.

I say hi to a few people and scan the room. God, is Chloe *still* in the car? And also, where's Tex? He was just right next to me and now, poof, disappeared. But then an elbow bumps my elbow. It's Tex, handing me a red cup full of beer.

"Here," Tex says.

"That was fast," I say.

We cheer cups, red plastic lip kissing red plastic lip. Beer is basically gross soda to me, so I take the tiniest sip in the world. After just a couple songs, the living room and kitchen are way thicker with people. We make our way through the crowd, toward the front door, to a staircase that leads downstairs.

Down here it's the perfect make-out den. It's quiet, just us, some kind of movie-viewing room with wall-to-wall shelves of DVDs. We read the titles and talk about what we've seen or haven't seen, laugh at stupid covers. I'm starting to feel slightly drunk, you know, giggling more than usual. I let him slip his arm around my waist for a moment as he talks passionately about the plot of *Rebel Without a Cause*. But then the arm drops off like he never even noticed it was there. The more he teases me, the more certain I am I want him. I definitely want him. I want him so bad it's driving me a little bit crazy right now.

He sips his beer and dances a half-joking butt-wiggle, hand in the air.

"Nice moves," I say.

"Let's see yours."

"Maybe in a little bit."

"You can't bring me to a party and not dance with me," he says.

I stare at his dreamy zombie face, that flirty smile on his lips. My pulse is racing. And whoa. I could maybe fall for you.

It's weird to, *bam,* realize that about someone I've known since before his voice broke. Maybe it's the costume, or the fact his hair is that perfectly imperfect length that falls forward, messy, into his eyes. But even though I know this is Tex Dell, the guy who lived on the next block from me and who I went to grade school with, he seems like a glorious stranger, one who makes my breath a little short.

"Come on," he says, tugging my sleeve. "Dance with me."

Like I could turn that offer down. So we go upstairs and dance. I don't even like this song, but I drink my beer and step to the beat, and when Tex's arm rubs against mine, my legs get noodly. I might as well be high on drugs when he gives me that stare, like there's no one else in the room, like the music thumps and hums for just us.

"Want to go outside?" Tex asks when the song's over.

"Sure," I say.

I am the sweatiest girl who ever lived.

We go through the kitchen, where Layla (dressed as Tinkerbell, in a skimpy outfit that matches the stripe in her hair) says "Hiiiiiii" to Tex and winks at me. We pass someone with a clown mask pureeing something pink in a blender. A gorilla's making out with a mouse near the pantry. Tex opens the sliding glass door to go out back. Here, the air is crisp and breezy, and the lights of the town are sleepy little candles. Tex slides the door shut, quieting the throbbing heartbeat of the techno music. It's just us out here.

"Wow," Tex grins. "Halloween's definitely my favorite holiday."

"Mine too," I say.

Well, it's actually Christmas. But tonight feels so magical that I just might change my mind.

My phone vibrates in my purse and I take it out.

Sorry we left, Chloe says. *Long story. Can you guys find a ride home?*

All the tingly happiness I felt a second ago from dancing and passing through the funhouse of a Halloween party freezes. Chloe ditched us? What the hell?

"Chloe left," I mutter.

I put my phone back. Her text doesn't even deserve an answer.

"Where'd she go?"

"She didn't say." I sigh. "God, that pisses me off. She's been so weird lately."

"You mean the bleached hair and the fake tan?"

"Well, yeah, that's weird, but it's bigger than that. It's like she doesn't want to hang out with me anymore."

"I'm sure it has nothing to do with you," he says.

"How do *you* know?"

"Because," he says, sipping. "You're the best. Everyone knows that."

Um . . . wow. "The best." What kind of best—*let's make out* best? Platonic friend best? I stare at his profile and determine that he has an impeccable chin. Yeah. A cleft chin. I never thought I could be so attracted to a freaking chin.

We sip and stare at the stars. We're on a wide deck that overlooks the rest of the yard: pool, Jacuzzi, lemon trees. I want to enjoy this night, I want to savor every moment with him here, but it's hard to not be annoyed at Chloe. Does she just not like me anymore? Does—what the . . . I have a strange feeling in the back of my pants and look up. Tex is pulling my tail.

"Stop," I laugh, and bat him away.

"Here, kitty-kitty," he says.

The light's dim out here, but that half-smile, that I'm-trying-not-to-smile smile, is undeniably flirty.

"I'm here already," I say.

He hides his made-up face in his red cup. He watches me as he drinks. His multicolored eyes make me lose myself; they really do. He scoots closer, right next to me. We lean on the railing and listen to the beat of the muffled music and stare at the moon.

"In some cases, the moon is you," he says.

I'm not sure if he's kidding. I'm not even sure what that *means*. I think hard but . . . nope. Nada. Zip.

"Huh?" I ask, finally.

"In any case, the moon."

"What are you *talking* about?" I laugh. "Shakespeare or something?"

"Jack Kerouac."

"Ahhh. That beatnik guy?"

"That beatnik guy," he says, fighting a smile.

I don't even know that much about beatniks, except they did drugs and were like, hippies, or something. I realize I know hardly anything about Tex and the things he's into—I mean, who guessed beatniks? The way he looks up at the moon, his eyes flickering, makes me wonder about what's inside that head of his. I wish I could peek and know everything without having to ask dumb questions.

"Layla. Tinkerbell in there," I say. "She was eyeing you earlier."

I don't know why I say it. I tell myself to stop—I know I'm just trying to get a feel for how he thinks of *me*—but my nervous lips keep flapping.

"How flattering," he says.

"It is flattering!" I say. "She's cute."

I don't really think she's cute. I mean, she's okay. I don't want *him* to think she's cute. But maybe I'll be able to figure out if this right here is actually *a date,* or who he's attracted to (me? please say me) if I tease him about girls.

"She's okay," he says.

"You should go for her."

He looks at me, an amused half-smile on his lips. Even the way he *slouches* seems irresistible to me somehow. Is it a full moon or something? Geez.

"You think so, huh?" he asks.

"Sure, why not?"

"Well, if that's what you want me to do . . ." He tilts his head back and drinks the rest of the beer.

"Only if you want to," I say quickly.

"Hmmm." He stares at me. He reaches out and puts his finger to my nose—my eyeliner-drawn cat nose. "Do I want to?"

"Do you?" I ask.

Okay. Whoa. I'm no stats buff, but the way he's staring at me now? I would have to say that the probability of a first kiss is near a hundred percent. And wouldn't that be the most epic first kiss right now, Halloween, with our silly makeup on, and the moon on full blast? In a mansion overlooking the city?

Someday we could be telling our kids this story. All right, all right. Maybe I'm getting just a little bit ahead of myself.

"Purr," he says.

I put my tongue behind my teeth and try, but I sound like a sputtering engine. I double over, but he's still looking at me, so serious, without a hint of humor in his voice.

"Purr, little kitty, purr," he says.

I try again, my tongue tucked in my mouth, and roll the sound along the back of my teeth.

We stare at each other. The crickets chirp; the music shakes; the voices and shrieks continue inside. But right now, in this moment, none of those sounds matters. I'm in a glass room made just for Tex and me. And his gaze, so full of—of some odd mix of sadness, and want, and fascination—it paralyzes me. I can't move. I really can't.

The sliding glass door opens behind us and we both startle, turning around. The special moment melts; our glass room shatters. It's a loud couple of girls tripping over their stilettos and sloshing beer on the patio as they stumble out to stand next to us. I recognize them from school but don't know their names. The short-haired brunette is dressed as a she-devil who's basically wearing a pair of glorified underpants over her fishnets, and the shock-blond in the leopard-print dress is painted blue.

"Party!" the she-devil yells at us, cheers-ing her red cup to no one.

"Meow." The blond makes a tiger-clawing-the-air motion with her red fingernails.

Tex just stares back at the blond—stares so hard I've become invisible beside him. Maybe he knows her. Or maybe he's thinking of how hot she looks in a leather jacket and skintight dress, even if she is painted blue. I tell the disappointment in my chest to stop spreading.

"Who are you?" he asks her.

"I'm Adelle," she says, surprised. "I'm in your first period."

"No, I mean, what are you supposed to be?"

"I'm a dead girl," she squeals happily, spinning around in her ankle boots.

Her friend laughs.

Tex doesn't move for a second, and even though his blinkless eyes say nothing, it clicks. Oh. I see what's happening now. And then he drops his cup at his feet and walks inside, back to the music, and leaves me staring at the two dumbfounded girls.

"He must be loaded," the blond giggles.

"Adelle," the she-devil says, pulling the blond's sleeve. "That's that dead girl's brother."

"Really? Shit. Well, how was I supposed to know that he'd be here?"

I turn and go inside, scanning the kitchen for Tex—nope. I stand smashed against a wall in the sweaty, pulsating living room and my eyes seek out a green-skinned boy. Not here, either. I go back downstairs to the den and find Tex there, behind the closed door. He's by himself on the couch, chewing the inside of his cheek. I sit on the couch and leave enough space for the ghost between us.

"I'm sorry," I say.

"Ha-ha, funny, dead girl," is all he says.

"It sucks."

"I should have done more."

"What can you do? It was a stupid costume."

"Not for *her*," he says bitterly. "For Perdita."

Her name—three syllables made of stone.

"It's only natural to feel, you know . . . like you could have saved her," I say softly. "But it was an accident."

He swallows like it hurts. "It wasn't an accident. She killed herself."

Those words weigh more than bricks.

Bam.

She. Killed. Herself.

How could he *know* that?

Why does he sound so *sure*?

"Sorry," I whisper.

"Everyone knows," he says flatly. "It's nothing new. She had Virginia Woolf and Sylvia Plath books on her bed when she died. She had cut up her arms the month before. It doesn't take a rocket scientist."

His eyes are watering. A tear, a clear tear, is rivering down his face, creating a flesh-colored line in the middle of his zombie makeup.

"Tell me," I say, shaking his knee, wanting him to look at me.

He shakes his head. "I can't."

"It's always good to talk about things," I say.

"No."

"Really, you can trust me."

"Some things you never tell anyone. You never talk about them." He opens his eyes and finally, *finally*, looks at me. His beautiful eyes are bloodshot. And I feel like a door between us just blew shut. It's done.

No kisses.

"Okay," I say quietly. "I'm sorry to bother you. I just want to help—"

"I know you do," he cuts in. "Thank you. Thank you for wanting to."

We call a cab to take us home. As we sit in the back seat, in the silence, black trees whip by the window and I watch him. He smiles at me, weakly, and I smile back.

As the cab pulls in front of Tex's, I look behind us, at the dark brambles of rosebushes surrounding his neighbor's house.

He gets out of the car and it's not just his makeup anymore. His expression, his posture, it all screams *zombie*.

We say goodnight and he walks up to his door. I might as well be watching a complete stranger. I swear I know less about him than I did that day when he first stared at me and turned me into the Girl Made of Glass.

"Heavy conversation, dude," the cab driver says, pulling away from the Dells' house.

The moon shines through my window, a diamond third eye superimposed over my inky reflection, and I think, if only I had a time machine.

CHAPTER 11

PROVE IT TO THEM

N OW THAT OUR SCENES ARE OVER in Theater, Pierre assigns us monologues Monday, which we're supposed to perform in front of everyone and their mom (literally) at some Theater Celebration night before Thanksgiving break. Kill me now, please. That's three weeks away!

I'd like to stomp on Chloe's pedicured foot. Because the fact I'm even in this class is all her fault. But she just studies her paper as she sits next to me in her seat. I can't help but notice the paper shaking a little in her hand, like she drank too much espresso, or skipped breakfast and/or lunch again. Her monologue says "Blanche, *A Streetcar Named Desire*," and she's mouthing the words to herself as she reads. The whole class is hushed as everyone studies their monologues for the first time. Tex, sitting way down the row, hasn't made eye contact with me today.

So, according to this piece of paper Pierre handed me a few minutes ago, I'm Emily, a girl from some old play called *Our*

Town. I can't help but think of Emily, my sister's less-than-charming friend, a cross between the ultimate dork and the ultimate snob (which are two things I never thought would go together until I met her). Performing in front of strangers! People's parents and friends. I could puke.

"I seriously regret you making me take this class," I whisper to Chloe.

"I didn't make you do anything," she whispers back without moving her gaze from her paper.

"I suck at memorizing things."

"Sorry you suck. Is that my fault?"

Ouch. Yesterday Chloe texted and apologized about Halloween, said she and Brody had to go "work things out" and she hoped I wasn't mad at her. But the icy tone in her voice almost makes me think she's mad at *me*.

"Did I do something?" I ask.

"What? No."

"You seem mad."

"Sorry. I'm not." She puts a stringy piece of bleach-blond hair behind her ear. "It's just—stop complaining about this class. At least you aced your first scene and got to flirt with a guy you liked while you were at it. Have you ever gotten an A on anything before? You should be thanking me."

I have to will my mouth to shut and not start arguing, because of Chloe's *tone*. What crawled up her butt and died?

"Chloe, why don't you move seats and sit up here?" Pierre eyes us with his hawk-stare through his rimless glasses. "You seem *distracted*."

I'm sure she hates me even more now. Pierre seems to kind of have it in for Chloe lately. She huffs a sigh and opens her binder to stick her monologue inside, and I notice an essay sitting there with a fat screaming red "C–" etched in pen and the words *You are capable of better than this!* double-underlined.

She slaps her binder shut, grabs her bookbag, and moves up to the front. Her skirt is so short I almost see her underwear as she walks away. I don't know what's more baffling—a C– on Chloe's paper—or the hoochie-mama skirt. But as she sits in front and flips her blond hair, I stare at the back of her head and think, *if I saw you right now, from this angle, I wouldn't even know who you are.* And that's something between sad and scary to realize. It's as if all these people around me have turned into ghosts and I'm suddenly alone on this planet. A lump in my throat sits there and even when I swallow, it won't go away.

That's when I feel that invisible tickle and turn to see Tex stare at me for one warm second before turning back to his paper. My pulse skips and I will my eyes back to my monologue. I wish I knew what he was thinking when he looked at me like that—the Girl Made of Glass look. I swear he can hear my thoughts.

When the bell rings, everyone hustles out of the room quickly, and we're the only ones left in the row.

"Arielle."

"Hey," I say.

"Walk with me," he says.

The way he says it, gently, but an order at the same time— gives me a joyful shiver. Even though he's not wearing zombie makeup, and I'm as sober as sober gets, when I let myself stare at him I still feel like I want to kiss him just as badly as I did on Halloween. It aches. It aches in this hopeful, beautiful, terrible way.

"Sure," I say, like, no biggie.

We walk to the exit together, up the stairs outside, and stand next to the bulletin board. I lean on it with my left shoulder, he with his right. There's about six inches between us. He smells minty, and just the scent of his mouth speeds up my blood pressure like crazy.

"I'm sorry," he says quietly.

I wave my hand in the air as if it hasn't been haunting me. "Oh, it's fine."

Then—*whoosh*.

Oh no . . . not now.

Not now, please, not now!

My ears ring, my heartbeat's loud as a bass drum, and I feel something, like, shrinking and growing at the same time. That good old déjà vu invades the conversation and widens the silence. I have a hard time responding for a second. I stare at him, frightened it's going to worsen—am I going to see ghosts *here, now*? I swallow and fix my eyes on his white T-shirt, where I swear I can see his heart. I see his heart, aorta and ticking ventricles and all, crawl out of his chest and back into his skin in a split second's time. Then the feeling passes. The déjà vu fades and my ears stop ringing. He's still staring at me, waiting for my response.

God, what is wrong with me? "Sorry. What were you saying?"

"I want to call you," he says. "Is that okay? Would that be weird?"

"You know I moved, right? I don't live on the next block anymore."

"Whoa," he says. "No, I didn't know that." He shakes his head. "Just my luck."

I get lost for a half-second in the yellow parts of his turquoise eyes.

"No." I can't help the huge grin that spreads across my cheeks. I stare at my sneakers and then back up at him. "It wouldn't be weird."

We take our phones out and exchange numbers.

"I'm serious," he says. "I'm going to call you."

I can't believe this is happening. I know this is Tex—the same Tex I was in sixth grade with, the same Tex who lived on the next block for years—but right now he seems different.

He's someone else, he's a hot guy who rides a motorcycle and whose hair is just perfectly long, and he's asking for my number.

"That would be fun," I say.

And then the bell rings.

And it's right above our heads, so we both jump about a foot back and cover our ears.

"Ow," I yell when it's done.

"Holy shit, I think I just busted an eardrum," he says, glaring up at the bell.

The moment is over. And not only that, our vice principal Mrs. Perez is down the hallway with that bulldog look in her eyes, walking quickly toward us on her clicky heels, which means we're about to get lectured about tardies.

"I need to go to Trig," I say.

"Come over this weekend," he says quickly. "To my house. My parents are usually gone all day. We can work on our monologues and . . . talk."

"Sure," I say, waving. "Sounds good."

I sprint out of there—I would rather be in Trig right now than here getting barked at by a lady who always has lipstick on her teeth. And the fact I would choose Trig over anything says a heck of a lot.

When I slide into my seat—Mr. Hale doesn't even notice; he's bent over the projector today muttering curse words and asking why it won't turn on—I'm palpitating as if I just ran a marathon. At first I think, geez, how out of shape am I? I ran across one hall and a lawn to get here. But then it dawns on me it has nothing to do with physical activity. It's Tex. When my phone buzzes in my pocket, it's from a name that is appearing on my phone for the first time. And I smile when I see those three letters: T-E-X.

The message just says, *I am very lucky.*

Sometimes I'm glad no one can hear my thoughts. Because the throb of my heart, the loud pump of blood flooding through me, whispers, *It gushes sweet, it hurts pretty, I'm falling fast and hard.*

But the next day it's not Tex who calls, but Casey. Casey *never* calls me. Sometimes Mom or Dad hands me the phone and we talk, but call me directly? She hasn't done it once since she joined the Harvard club. So I'm almost suspicious when I pick up. Like, is someone dead? Or do you need a favor? But she says she just called to see how I'm doing.

"I'm . . . fine," I say.

I'm in the dining room. It's after school and I'm the only one home.

I sit at the table and stare at the vase of marbles, trying to shake my amazement that Casey's just calling to be friendly. College has seriously changed her.

"It's been forever since I talked to you," she says.

"Yeah, it's been a minute."

"How's junior year?"

"I think I'm suffering from an early case of senioritis. How's Harvard?"

"I'm living a dream. I feel so lucky to be here with so many amazing people and professors. Did Mom show you the pics I emailed?"

"Yeah," I say. "The campus looks pretty."

"My Shakespeare teacher is a bestselling author. I mean, he just published an essay in the *New Yorker*."

"Good for him," I say.

Oops. I didn't mean for that to come out so bitter.

"I mean, it must be cool to study with people like that," I correct myself.

"It's not just 'cool'; it's inspiring," she says.

There's a static silence.

"Um . . . so what's your major?"

"I'm not sure yet," she says. "I'm thinking if I study poli-sci but have some work experience in the legal field, I'll be prepped to run for office one day. First city council, eventually Congress, and then who knows? What do you think about that? Think I could become president?"

She's only half-kidding. Even though she's bragging up the wazoo, I haven't heard Casey sound so alive and happy since we were kids. It's almost eerie.

"What about Emily?" I ask. "How's she doing?"

"Emily?" she asks, as if she has no idea who I'm talking about. "Oh—oh God, she and I aren't even in contact anymore. I haven't seen her since the first week of school."

"That sucks," I say.

"Not really," she says. "She's—different now. I went to her Facebook page a month or so ago and I barely even recognized her."

"How so?"

"Oh, she cut her hair and dyed it jet black just like Bettie Page," she says. "No glasses anymore. Red lipstick. I don't know. Major makeover, I guess. It's weird how fast some people change."

"Yeah," I say, twisting my hair with one hand and letting it go. "You know who looks like a totally different human now?"

"Who?"

"Chloe," I say.

"How?" she asks.

"She lost a bunch of weight, bleached her hair, and dresses different. Kind of slutty. Oh, and she got a spray tan."

Then Casey says, "I miss you."

Those words—coming from the girl who used to be enemy number one living under my own roof—shock me and sink in with special meaning.

"You too," I say. "Thanks for calling."

When I hang up, I stare at my phone. Something about that short conversation stretched my years forward and backward—made me feel both nostalgic and old.

I stand up and look at the table, at the newspaper I smoothed out during the conversation. There's a story about some boring political race. I flip the paper over and my blood immediately freezes when I spot the headline near the bottom of the page next to that all-too-familiar senior portrait of Perdita.

DROWNED GIRL'S AUTOPSY REPORT IN— FOUL PLAY SUSPECTED

Autopsy results from the death of eighteen-year-old Perdita Dell, local girl found drowned in Lake Los Caballos in August, have revealed findings that cause police to now suspect foul play as a possibility in her death.

According to the report, cause of death remains asphyxiation from drowning. However, a patch of missing hair from the head of the victim, along with unidentified DNA under the fingernails, has led police to believe the death is more than a simple accident or suicide as they previously thought.

"The case is still open," Detective Lopez, who has been leading the investigation, told local press at a conference Monday afternoon. "We're entertaining all possibilities at this point, although we don't have a suspect. The department is doing everything to try to solve the question of what happened to this girl. We urge anyone with any information at all to please contact the department directly and even leave an anonymous tip."

Foul play?

What exactly is "foul play"?

Is that . . . *murder?*

My knees feel weak. A patch of missing hair. Someone's DNA under her fingernails—as in, she was scratching and fighting with someone? But what Tex said about suicide. . . he sounded so convinced. Look at me: I'm standing in the dim dining room, hyperventilating as I hover over the newspaper. I want to bawl, imagining that someone did that to Perdita. I could call my sister—wouldn't she want to know? But she sounded so happy, and I don't want to ruin that. Besides, what can she do? She's thousands of miles away. If she knew anything, she would have told the police when they talked to her.

I'm so sad tonight, thinking about murder—murder! Murder, across the street from my house, someone *murdered* my sister's best friend, my would-be-boyfriend's big sister—that I am queasy like I've got food poisoning.

As if that's not bad enough, believe me—it gets worse.

Like I just said, I don't feel well, so I go to bed kinda early, before my parents even get home from their date. And because I went to bed so early, I wake up super early, before the sun, and lie there for a long time in bed before deciding to just get up and shower and ready myself for school an hour early. I go to the bathroom, turn on the shower, pull my pajamas off, and then in the mirror I see just about the creepiest sight I've seen since the skeleton girl paid me her last visit.

135

On my belly, there are long scratch marks, raised and pink, like some horrid animal or person scratched me. Eight of them. Long, nearly bloody, stretching from right beneath my boobs to past my belly button.

I gasp when I see them. I grab onto the counter for a sec before staring again and touching them to make sure they're real. Yes, they are. Tender and a bit painful, and fresh.

All I can think of—and I realize this is a dire conclusion, but hello! I'm creeped out!—is that scene in that scary-as-hell old movie *The Exorcist* where she has "Help me" written on her stomach. Now, I don't believe in the devil. I know I'm not possessed. But I do believe in ghosts. And the fact that yesterday I read the news that Perdita was probably murdered and that she had DNA under her fingernails—and now I wake up with unexplained scratches all over my belly, like a ghost took her fingernails to my skin and scratched me in the night—that fact is not lost on me. I know that's what this is.

I've been scratched by a ghost, I think, watching my reflection in the mirror disappear in the fog of the shower steam. And why? I can think of only two reasons. The first is that she's trying to tell me something. Maybe she wants me to help solve her murder—I don't know, I'm just throwing ideas out there, okay? The second reason is one I don't let myself think about too long. That it is a warning from the afterlife. This is a ghost reaching at me with her long fingernails, saying, *You're next.*

I never thought it was possible to shiver in a hot shower, but I've learned something new today.

When I go back to my room and get ready for school, I think back to those tips I read months ago about seeing ghosts. I remember that book I saw with the Specter of Newby Church. And an idea comes to me—I'm going to start recording everything that happens in my room while I sleep.

Why didn't I think of that before?

Just set up my computer and boom—film it.

Because some kind of spirit has so far knocked over my furniture, broken my lamp, and now scratched me in the night. I know if I tell people, they'll think I'm nuts, because it sounds nuts. But I know it's true and real.

And I'm going to prove it to them.

CHAPTER 12
THE OTHER DIRECTION

Mmm-ch. Mmm-ch. Mmm-ch. My inner techno beat is turned to eleven.

I don't know why my heartbeat is going nuts—am I more nervous to hang out with Tex alone, or to step foot in Perdita's house? As I walk up the cement stones that lead to the Dells' front door, I can't help but bend my neck upward to catch a glimpse of her window, half-expecting to see a platinum-haired ghost.

I ring the doorbell, sounding far-off chimes. Don't think about Perdita and the whole murder thing, I'm telling myself. But of course, the very thought makes it impossible. Still, I can't deny this smile when the door opens and that stare-right-through-you gaze is aimed straight at me.

"What's up?" Tex says.

His hair is wet, slicked back, like he just stepped out of the shower. I smell aftershave.

"Your hair looks pretty," he says. "I like it up like that."

"I didn't brush it, just for you."

He bites a lip that I can tell wants to smile.

I step inside, fluttering a little.

I've never been inside this house before, I realize. He gives me a quick tour, padding around the cream-colored carpet with its fresh vacuum tracks. It's laid out the same but cleaner and definitely fancier than my old house, light pouring in everywhere upstairs through skylights, but it feels empty, untouched somehow. His parents aren't home. Their master bedroom looks like a hotel suite, drapes that match the bedspread. And there's one door upstairs that he stops in front of.

"This is her room," he says simply, hand on the doorknob. "Or, you know, *was*."

"Huh."

I get this weird swishy feeling on my neck, like I just let my hair down. But I didn't. I pinned it up old-school Chloe-style before I came. Shiver.

He doesn't open the door, but keeps his hand there. "It's weird in there. Wanna see?"

I shrug. I kind of don't, to be honest—or maybe I do. Maybe I do and I'm just scared. But scared why? She's just Perdita. She's just my sister's dead friend.

"Eh, maybe later," he says, and heads into his room.

Tex's room smells of air freshener, which is pretty much the opposite of how Conrad's room used to smell: dirty laundry and potato chips. Tex's room is where Casey's would be in my house, only his is painted blue and his bed is in the opposite corner. He has just one poster of a Harley on his wall, not famous basketball players and girls in bikinis à la Conrad.

His black futon is made. There's a beaten-up book that says *Howl* on his pillowcase.

"So this is my room," he says in a silly valley-girl voice, collapsing into a sitting position on his bed.

I laugh. "Totally rad, man," I answer in a valley-girl voice of my own.

I sit next to him, but not too close. Even though he almost smooched me before sixth period this week, it's strange to just be in someone's house when you've barely known him for years, to suddenly cross that boundary and peek inside. And then there's the fact this boy shares DNA with a girl who the paper said was murdered this week. He hasn't mentioned it, but it must be on his mind. I mean, there's a big difference between murder and suicide. I won't lie, he gives me butterflies, but this is semi-weird.

"How are things?" I ask, when what I really mean is, how are you holding up knowing it's possible someone out there killed your sister?

"Things are . . . on one hand, things are great. I'm here with you, right?"

"What about the other hand?"

His face goes blank and his smile disappears. "You saw the paper."

"Yeah."

"I don't know, my head is spinning."

"I'll bet."

"Does Casey know?"

"Not yet, I don't think so."

"I just can't believe anything anybody tells me anymore," he says.

"How are your parents?"

"Oh, they're pissed," he says. "Or my mom's pissed. She threatened to sue the police. She's been saying someone killed Perdita all along. I guess that's easier to believe than accepting the fact she probably killed herself."

"It's really sad," I say. "I wish Perdita could tell us what happened."

As the words escape my mouth, I'm afraid they sound dumb, or reveal too much. Like how I've been worried about the scratch marks on my belly and videoing myself sleeping every night.

"All we have now are wishes," he says after a moment, his eyes glued to me. It's like he sees underneath my skin. Sees my brain working, my emotions swirling. I've never been around someone who made me feel this way.

My lips slacken and—who knows, could be the watermelon balm I wore—but I can tell he's watching them. I wonder if he's going to finally kiss me. That's how it was with Conrad: the first day he invited me over to "study for Spanish" he was all over me the second he shut his bedroom door. I got a D in Spanish that semester.

I want Tex to kiss me so bad it's a hunger. I haven't been kissed in months, and his face only gets better the more I stare at it.

Then my heart *mmm-ch*s again and my mind's like *Perdita Perdita Perdita* and I feel her nothingness everywhere. I can remember the sound of her laugh, through a wall. I can imagine hearing her right now, and my stomach stirs.

"She's dead," he says. "End of story."

The way he says it, so blasé, is jarring.

I get up and look out his window, down into their back yard, where sprinklers sparkle the green lawn. One thing that's different about their house? They've got a swimming pool. Luckies. But then my skin crawls a little.

Seems extra tragic that a girl with her own swimming pool drowned in a shallow lake.

And I get this sinking *oh yeah*ness. All the smitten kiss-me hope of five minutes ago is instantly dredged with this yucky memory of Perdita's body. The way her arms hung limp. My smile melts, my body gets like ten times heavier, and I realize

142

the barriers. Tex and I—as much as I want him, as freaking heavenly as a kiss would be—we can just never for a million reasons. There's too much in the way.

"You okay?" he asks, standing behind me.

I jump a little. "Oh. Yeah. Just looking at your pool."

"Nobody's used it since August."

A part of me wants to ask him, do you know? Do you know I saw her body? I never told him that part.

His mouth is a straight line and I notice him swallow.

"I'm sorry," I say.

"Why?"

"Because . . ."

"It's not your fault, it has nothing to do with you, so don't be sorry. Anyway," he says, "I've bummed you out. This really isn't how I was hoping today would go."

"No, I—"

"You've got a look on your face like a kid who lost her puppy."

And then he puts his hands on my waist.

There is serious electricity flooding over me. I'm confused. There is so much going on right now in me. I saw his dead sister's body; his dead sister was my sister's best friend once; I want to make out with him; I would like his tongue in my mouth right now.

Pierre talks about conflict in Theater. The tension that makes a scene so good. Well, come on! This is some serious conflict.

I close my eyes for a second, my ears ringing—not now, body; don't pull this weird dizzy thing on me now.

"Something wrong?" he asks. His arms drop from my waist.

"Fine," I say, swallowing once, twice. "I'm lightheaded."

"The heat?" he asks. "It is ridiculous for November."

"Yeah." I smile. "I'll be fine."

It lifts, the weirdness, and I silently thank my body.

"How about we . . ." he starts.

Start kissing? Never talk of death again? Get married and run away together and have fat babies?

". . . go for a swim? Maybe it'll cool you off."

"Seriously?" I ask after a second.

"Yeah," he says. "It's hot as shit, or is it just me?"

"I don't have a suit, though."

"You can wear one of her suits." He points to the wall toward Perdita's room. He says it so casually, like she's just away for the afternoon or something.

My mouth goes kind of dry as I imagine wearing a dead girl's swimsuit and swimming in a dead girl's pool. Perdita's room is behind that motorcycle poster and behind that wall. Perdita. The girl who I thought was the coolest chick ever, the dead girl I have been semi-obsessed with for months now, the girl whose ghost is possibly haunting me and scaring me on a regular basis. So. I feel bonded to her, you know? I want to see her room and all its things, to touch her swimsuit, to fill this loss in the air with something real and human.

"All right," I say. "Sure."

I can't believe I'm doing this, but I follow Tex to Perdita's room. He doesn't linger in front of her door this time. He pushes it straight open and as I walk in, I get a lukewarm shock. A bodily weirdness. A dose of déjà vu. And then it sinks in . . . I'm here. In a room that is, layout-wise, an exact replica of my room. Only it's Perdita's.

Perdita's.

What can I say . . . it's creepy. It's magical. *Bam!* I've stepped into another world. Black canopy bed, sea-green walls, a giant *Alice in Wonderland* poster. But there's this smell in here, a faint vanilla that almost brings tears to my eyes. *I know that smell.* So well it stings my throat. It was a smell that lingered in Casey's room after their slumber parties. Perdita's closet, open, is a rainbow of dresses, with heels and boots scattered over the carpet. Her bras dangle from her canopy. I mean, this feels like a room she just left. My skin buzzes with all the her that isn't here, with the sum of these things that now equal what is left of Perdita.

Her leather jacket—the one I've seen for years, with the fist-shaped bloody heart patch sewn to the back—stares at me from the floor.

"So weird to see that without her in it," I say.

"I hate that jacket. It's creepy," he says. "Like a ghost that can't move."

"Why do you say that?"

"That jacket and the patch used to belong to my aunt," he says. "She died of cancer a few years ago and gave it to Perdita before she passed. They were close. Perdita said it made her feel like Aunt Rita was still alive, like she carried a piece of her everywhere. Perdita got a necklace of a heart, too, like the patch."

"Yeah, I know that necklace."

"Now she's dead like Aunt Rita."

"It's not the *jacket's* fault."

He eyes it there on the floor with suspicion. "When Aunt Rita died, and Perdita inherited the jacket, it was like—I don't know, it was like she tried to act as if she'd inherited more than a stupid jacket or something. She toughened up the way Aunt Rita was, too cool for everyone, a little bit bad. Perdita thought people live on in the things they leave behind—that things can keep speaking when people are long gone. A heart patch lasts longer than a heart."

"You disagree?"

"I don't know. Maybe. If they do, it's sad. It's just sad that stuff outlives us."

I have to swallow to not start choking up.

"No one ever comes in here," Tex says.

I don't say a word, afraid I'll sputter into tears or something.

"Actually, I'm lying. I've come in here before," he goes on, sticking his hands in his pockets. "But I never touch anything."

I breathe in, one-two-three, to slow the burn in my throat.

"I know. Is this crazy, or what? Is my family fucked in the head, or what?"

I wipe my eyes. Stupid tears. Her own brother isn't crying, so why should I?

"I can still smell her in here," he goes on. "Not her; this body spray she wore."

My lips part, my mouth searches for a word, but I just don't know what to say.

"We hated each other, Arielle. Like serious hatred. I'm not sad she's gone; I'm just angry and confused. You don't need to keep staring at me like that—like I'm some broken thing that needs fixing."

What he just said is so surprising, it knocks the breath out of me for a moment.

"I know your brother drowned, too," he says softly. "But you actually got along with him. It's different when a selfish asshole you didn't get along with dies."

"But she was your sister," I say.

"She was. And I wish she wasn't dead now. But she wasn't a saint."

I gulp. What am I supposed to say to that? I get a chill the way he says it, so point-blank. That he hated his dead sister.

I stare at her dresser top, the face creams and safety pins and rolling papers, the half-eaten bag of sunflower seeds and used tissues. With each, I can imagine Perdita—that sassy-mouthed bottle-blond fashionista Perdita—*putting* it there. I can see her crumpling a receipt and carelessly dropping it, see her knock over her nail polish bottles so they lie in a dead little line, see her shrug off her jacket and let it slither to the floor before crawling into bed. You can still trace the shape where her body lay in her pink sheets, where she pushed the comforter back to get out of bed on that last day of her life.

Tex stares at me staring at her room. Right now, I wish he wouldn't. I don't want to be the Girl Made of Glass right now.

I make myself smile at him. "Maybe we shouldn't swim."

"Why not, Arielle?"

Ugh. What is it about this boy?

"It's just weird," I say. "Wearing her bathing suit."

"It's not sacred," he says. "Don't be like my parents and think that way—that these *things* are *her*. Besides, if Perdita were here, I know she wouldn't give two shits about whether or not you borrowed a suit from her."

Tex heads to her dresser, carefully stepping over her leather jacket. He tosses a black one-piece to me and I catch it with both hands.

"Go ahead and change in here," he says.

"Okay."

He closes the door behind him, and here I stand, alone, in the middle of the tornado of Perdita's things. I look around, half-expecting to see a shadow, a ghost, dear God please not a skeleton girl, but it's so undeniably still in here. And the techno-blast that is my heartbeat returns. I shuck my clothes off and slip into the suit, pulling it up over my fading pink belly-scratches. I tie the halter around my neck and glance in the mirror on her closed door. It fits. It's pinup pretty. I look unlike myself.

That's when I can't move for a second, eyes glued to the mirror. Because that eerie feeling I've had returns. It's so hard to explain. It's just like, I've done this before. This has already happened. I'm watching a rerun. I've been in this room in this suit on this day before. And this time, it's mixed with a little panic. Because I'm seriously afraid that I'm going to see her ghost. I step forward and stand near her door. Take some deep breaths with my hand on the doorknob. Look up at the pictures and postcards taped to her doorframe. A punk girl with black lipstick whose name I don't know. Sid Vicious. Black-and-white lines of chorus girls. Some glossies of her friends at parties, a group of kids on the beach. I don't recognize any of them. And as I gaze at one of the pics—I know how bizarre this sounds, so please bear with me—in one flash of a second, little flowers seem to grow out of the eyeholes and mouth holes of these people in the pictures. Tiny roses that appear and disappear within a blink's time. It happens so fast that when I do a double-take, they're not there. And then I feel a tap on my shoulder, a *pssst* tickles my ear, and I turn around.

"Whatcha lookin for?" a whisper deep inside my ear asks.

There's no one behind me. I stare at Perdita's room and reach up and touch my left ear, where I swear I just heard that voice.

Tex knocks on the door. "You decent?"

"Yeah," I squeak.

Pull yourself together, Arielle. Imagination. That's what you've got, an imagination.

I open up the door.

There he stands in board shorts. Tex's body is, um . . .

He hands me a towel and I wrap it around my waist. I follow him to the pool. He cannonballs in; I do a swan dive. I haven't been in a pool in months, and it's obscenely hot for November. With water drizzling down his face and his hair all slicked back, I have to will myself to stop staring at Tex as I splash around.

"The pool's nice," I say.

His mouth, all wet and dripping, is inches from mine. I want to kiss him and yet I'm still shaky from my weird vision upstairs. To escape his stare, I dive down and sit at the bottom of the pool for a moment, holding my breath, closing my eyes, and I disappear.

I, Arielle, am no more for a moment, and it feels beautiful.

Then I surface again, inhale and exhale, and open my eyes. Perdita, dead in the lake. Ghosts I can't prove. Tex is still watching me as he treads water and I want to tell him something, anything. Get rid of this nauseous guilt, share it with someone. He comes closer and his wet face is next to mine. My heart is a hammer.

"What are you looking so solemn for?" he asks.

I have to will myself to not hyperventilate from his nearness.

"I don't know."

He gives me that serious turn-you-to-mush stare. I shouldn't do it. But because he watches me like I'm the only girl on planet Earth, and because I want him so bad my bones scream, and because I want to plug my fingers in my ears and say lalalalala and not think about Perdita and not think about death and the dark and horrors—and, okay, also because he's the hottest guy I've jumped in a pool with EVER—I put my hand on his cheekbone, and draw that irresistible mouth to mine.

He pulls me closer and opens his mouth, kisses me so softly, so surprisingly softly. And everything disappears except the feeling. Finally, after a tiny eternity, he pulls away. I laugh and wipe my mouth, tasting his fruity Chapstick and chlorine.

"I've wanted that for months," he says.

"So why didn't you?" I ask.

He shakes his head. "You're too good for me."

"Don't say that."

"You are," he says. "You're perfect. And I'm a mess. Believe me, I only show you the best parts."

He's not making eye contact with me anymore. He's staring at the flickering blue of the water.

"Everyone's like that. I have secrets, too," I tell him, thinking of the skeleton girl. What a relief to utter those words.

"Yeah, I'm sure."

"I do!" I say.

But then there's a weird springy noise from behind us. Tex splashes a foot away. I turn around. That warmth I felt just a second ago shrivels into this yucky shame as I see the outline of a figure peeping through the side fence at us.

The shadow of a fat man in a hat. Just standing there, not moving. Staring at us like a total creeper!

"What the hell? What is he *doing*?" I whisper.

"Being a perv. Doing what he does. The Judge used to stare at Perdita all the time. She even saw him using binoculars to look up in her window once."

"Gross," I say, and I honestly want to gag.

And he's still doing it! The neighbor's just pressed up against the fence, watching us with total shamelessness.

"I'm done," I say. "I want to go inside."

"Hey, fucker," Tex yells. "You ruined it. I had a beautiful girl in a pool on a sunny afternoon and you blew it."

Tex and I get out, grab towels, and head inside.

"You should report him," I say, toweling off in the kitchen.

Tex looks pissed. "He used to be a judge. He's buddy-buddy with every cop in town."

"It's so *gross*," I say. "All peeping-Tom-style."

"No shit." He sighs. He's watching me with this sorry look. And the moment's so busted. "You can change in her room, leave the bathing suit hanging in the bathroom."

"Okay," I say.

I head upstairs, defeated.

Back in her room, I change quickly. And this is when I do something I'm not proud of, I open her top drawer just to peek inside. There's a mess of hair clips, highlighters, random papers. A tampon box with a bunch of cash inside. I don't stop to count it or anything, that seems too nosy, but it looks like a lot. I pick up a paper mache heart-shaped box and open it. It has random dangly earrings inside, and I'm about to shut it when I hear that same whisper from before, in my left ear, deep inside—almost like it's in my own head.

"Under the bottom," it says. "Look."

I hesitate, watching myself in the mirror for a sec and not believing what I just heard. But my left ear is still buzzing. I press my finger to it to make the itch stop. And then I pull the velvet up at the bottom of the box. Nothing. It's stuck.

I flip the box over. There's still a price tag on it, though the ink has faded. I pull at the bottom and guess what? It comes off in my hand.

Secret compartment.

Inside, there's just a folded piece of notebook paper. It has a message written in red pen.

BITCH IF YOU DON'T GIVE ME WHAT I ASKED FOR YOUR LIFE AS YOU KNOW IT IS OVER

I suck in air like I've been slugged. What is this? A threat? Was someone threatening Perdita—was this written by the person who possibly hurt her? I stand there with the note trembling in my hand, not knowing what to do. Maybe I should tell Tex. But then I'd have to admit to snooping in his dead sister's belongings, which would make me the ultimate creep. Maybe I should call the police later. I put it carefully back into the bottom of the heart-shaped box, and fit the bottom back onto the box so the secret compartment is a secret again. The room dizzies a bit as my head swims, and wish I hadn't seen it.

That whisper.

I slide the drawer shut, guilty, catching a glimpse of my wide-eyed reflection in the dusty vanity mirror. I'm standing in a dead girl's room. A dead girl just whispered in my ear, and I might have just accidently seen a piece of evidence.

YOUR LIFE AS YOU KNOW IT IS OVER

When I come out of the room and head downstairs, Tex is standing in a T-shirt and swim trunks, wet hair glued to his face. He's an irresistible shade of California-boy caramel, and if I weren't feeling so distracted and sick, I would stay and make out with him some more.

"Are you mad at me?" he asks.

"No!" I say.

"You look . . . upset."

"I'm sorry," I say.

I reach out and touch his arm—and I can't believe he just lets me; it's still so weird to feel like I have permission to touch him.

"That asshole ruined it," he says, frowning.

"He didn't ruin anything."

Neither of us blinks. He reaches his hand up my arm and pulls me to him and kisses me, slow and warm and sweet, and I get lost for a minute in the gold nothingness of my closed eyes—until I remember what I saw in Perdita's drawer, and get that sick-with-guilt twist in my belly. I don't deserve to be kissed by him right now. I pull away.

"I need to go," I say. "Help my dad with something."

Lies, of course.

I step out, close the door, and walk across his lawn, my wet hair cooling me off. As I step onto the sidewalk, I see their neighbor in the front yard. It's Peeping Tom, the neighbor with the staring problem. His fat face is squared right on me and he's wearing that same hat as last time, shears in his hand, bending over some big fat red roses.

"His sister was easy, too," he says. "Be safe, now. Don't want to end up like her."

I stop in my tracks for a second. WHAT?!

But when I turn around, he's just whistling and trimming roses, facing the other direction.

CHAPTER 13
ARIELLE'S TERRIBLE, HORRIBLE, NO GOOD, VERY BAD DAY

EVEN IN NOVEMBER, some Velero Saturdays are sunkissed and beachworthy. But dream weather or not, I'd rather lie in bed all morning.

"Did you hear about Perdita?" Dad asks when I finally hit the kitchen up for breakfast. He's sitting at the dining room table with the newspaper open to the comics section.

"About the 'foul play' thing?" I ask.

He nods, closing the paper. "Very disturbing stuff."

"What I don't get is, if they have DNA, why can't they just run it through their computer or whatever and figure out who it belongs to?"

"It's probably not in the database."

"Does it really mean she was murdered?" I ask. "Her brother Tex told me she killed herself. She had Sylvia Plath and Virginia Woolf books on her bed—you know, suicidal writers."

"Looks more complicated than that." He shakes his head. "It's been worrying me. I mean, I have two girls. I think about this all the time. She died across the street from us! You think I don't worry every time you leave the house to go somewhere?"

"Dad."

"If she was killed, the person who did it is still out there."

"I'm really careful."

"Tell me you don't go to the lake anymore."

"I don't."

He gets up and hugs me. It takes me a sec to hug him back. My dad's a happy-go-lucky guy; I'm not used to him being angry, and definitely not used to him being scared. And that's what this is. Because of Perdita's death, my dad's scared for me. He probably has been for a while.

"It's okay," I tell him. "I'm really safe."

"I couldn't handle losing a daughter," he says.

I know there's more to that sentence. Something like *I already lost a son*. But he doesn't finish it.

"This is why you have curfews," he says into my shoulder.

"I know."

"I don't want anything like this to happen to you. You need to make the right choices," he says.

He pulls back to look at me.

"I do," I say.

"You okay?" Dad asks, rubbing my arm.

"Yeah," I say. "It's just really sad."

All at once, I see her, a mental movie clip: Perdita in that leather jacket, smiling her lipstick-bright smile at me, poking her head into my room to say hi.

She was so beautiful; she was so young.

My sister's best, best friend once.

Dead.

I wipe the tears away. "I promise I'll be safe."

I go back to my room, change my clothes a few times for no reason, watch five minutes of seven TV shows, and even try to study for a while, but I keep getting distracted.

I can't help but think of that gross neighbor staring at her with binoculars. Is that not the perviest thing ever? And it rings a few alarms. I've seen TV shows about creepy dudes who started off peeking in windows and ended up raping and killing women. It's not the most far-off hypothesis in the world.

Even though I should be studying my monologue, reading for English, or finishing Trig homework, instead I Google about Perdita. I know the Internet can't give me a satisfying answer, but maybe I can find some connection to that Judge guy who gives me such a creepy vibe. Nope. Nothing is written about the creeper next door. Also, doesn't exactly help that I don't have his name. There are just the two articles about Perdita in the local paper I already read. *Foul play.* Those two syllables raise the hairs on my neck. I keep thinking about those words penned in red, repeating them in my mind as if they could lead me somewhere. I imagine the Judge wrote them, the Judge was the one who bullied her on Facebook. Or maybe it was some random person. I just can't imagine anyone hating Perdita enough to do any of those things—to write the note, to threaten her online, and most especially, to kill her.

To rip hair from her head.

To scare her enough that she scratched him, that she had his DNA under her fingernails.

Sunday morning, I wake up on the floor. My neck hurts, a crick times a hundred, and I am totally confused as I stare at the ceiling. Of course, the first thought I have is that obviously last night a ghost—Perdita AKA the skeleton girl, I'm imagining—threw me off my bed. It sounds crazy, even just as a thought in my head. But I was recording myself last night. Now I can discover what happened for sure—if there really is a ghost tormenting me, I'm finally about to find out.

I sit down on my bed with my computer on my lap, careful not to move my neck, and look at the video file from last night. I scroll through it in fast motion, squinting at the screen, watching for spirit-like figures, flashes, anything out of the ordinary. But I'm just lying there. Every once in a while I turn or kick the blankets off, but that's it.

About two-thirds of the way through the footage, though, I see myself fall off the bed. I don't notice a ghost there when I watch it, but it's super sped up. So I slow down the video and go back to where I start moving.

The room is clear and dark. Nothing is in the air—not a smoke-like substance, not a skeleton girl, not a floating orb. It's just me there, in bed, and I suddenly start thrashing, my head moving up and down, my arms waving. I kick the blankets down to my feet and move so jerkily it's like I'm being choked by someone invisible. Then I just turn and fall right off the bed and go still.

That's it. Then I don't move, like I'm asleep.

It's the weirdest thing I've ever seen, and totally unsettling because that's *me* looking all possessed and crazy. I watch it over and over again, looking for a ghost.

"Oh shit," I whisper.

I text Chloe that afternoon.

I'm with Brody, she says. *We just got back from hot yoga. What's up?*

I don't harp on the "yoga" part, although I'm tempted. I hang up my phone, thinking, gee, thanks, Chloe. Her tone sounded like how Casey used to talk to me when she still lived at home. Like I was a total dweeb cramping her style.

While I wait for her to arrive, I try to figure out how I'm going to explain this to her. Do I start with the ghosts, how I think I've been seeing ghosts? Do I show her the video? Chloe knocks once on my door and comes in.

Her hair is freshly bleached and ponytailed. She's wearing a leopard-print sports bra and matching booty shorts. She's sweaty and looks grumpy. She puts her purse on the floor.

"Okay . . . what's going on?" She folds her arms. "Just FYI, you do realize it's noon, right? Most of the world is dressed by now."

Chloe's phone starts buzzing in her purse and she looks at it.

"Brody's coming back to pick me up," she says. "We're going to look at blenders."

Look at . . . blenders? She starts texting back and I get this sinking feeling, shrinking like a doll. I'm a child and Chloe is too old and cool and mature to talk to me.

"Remember how you used to be?" I ask. "You were a feminist."

"I'm still a feminist."

"You thought curvy women were beautiful."

She doesn't say anything.

"You thought blond chicks were generic."

She sighs. "Your point?"

"You've changed," I say.

"So?" she asks. "So what?"

"You used to talk crap about girls who dieted all the time and went to tanning salons and stuff."

"I changed my mind," she says.

"Yeah, funny how that happened right when you started dating a shallow bro who's obsessed with exercising."

"Wow—didn't know you felt that way," she says, stiffening.

"You don't eat enough and you're way meaner when you don't eat."

"I didn't realize you were a nutritionist—thanks for the advice. Coming from a girl who lives on pizza and Cheetos and lives in her stained pajamas."

My mouth falls open. I search for a comeback, but draw a blank.

Chloe checks her phone. "Oh," she says with a fake smile, holding it in the air. "My 'shallow bro' is here. Catch ya later!"

She slams the door after her.

I sit here on my bed, look down at my stained PJs, and even though I tell them not to—my eyes well up. My hands, in my lap, are shaking.

Chloe and I have been known to bicker, sure. We didn't speak for an hour during a sleepover once because I told her I thought a dress of hers was "grandma-ish." I hung up on her once because she said my voice could be "like someone who sucked a balloon" when I was excited about something. But we don't ever get in real fights. I can hardly believe that just happened.

Everything's unraveling at once, and I have no one to turn to. I look at myself in my mirror and decide I hate my stupid pajamas. I look like a slob. Screw this. I'm going to rifle through Casey's boxes and steal some of her matching pajamas.

I pass my dad at the dinner table, eating organic Fruit Loops.

"Hey kiddo," he says. "How's it hangin'?"

"I hate everything," I say.

He stares at me as I walk past him to the living room closet.

"Okay," he says cheerfully. "Any reason why?"

"Only about a million."

"What'cha lookin for?"

"I hate my stupid pajamas."

"Well, if you feel that way, you might want to think about getting dressed."

"I'm taking some of Casey's."

I go inside the closet and pull the light bulb's string. *Pop.* There are stacks of boxes in here, all labeled *CASEY.*

"I don't think she'd like that," Dad says.

Who cares about Casey—if she wanted her stuff so bad, she'd have taken it to Harvard. I lift a box off a stack and open it. It's mostly scarves, some old bathing suits, a couple thick, black leather binders. I take a scarf and contemplate the bathing suit, but it's faded and old-looking.

"Arielle," Dad's voice says from the kitchen.

I roll my eyes. "I'm just looking."

"She's coming back in a week and says she's shipping most of that stuff back to Cambridge," he says.

I open a binder, just out of curiosity.

Inside, there are Xeroxed pages separated by yellow tabbed dividers. The dividers say things like "Pre-Calc (Ms. Healy)," "Government (Mr. Melton)," and "English (Junior; Miss Jenkins)."

What the hell?

I flip through the pages and start realizing what's in my hands right now. They're tests. They're the teachers' versions of tests—and midterms. And finals. Photocopied. Über-organized.

All the blanks are filled with correct answers, written in different teachers' scrawls. I can't believe what I'm seeing.

There are seriously near a hundred pages like this.

I know there must be some explanation because Casey, the goody-two-shoes queen herself, would *never* cheat.

My stomach does a cartwheel and I nearly jump a foot when my dad almost yells, "Arielle, I'm serious!"

"Okay," I say, slamming the binder shut and returning it to the box. "Geez."

I close the box back up and put it back. I shut the closet door. My dad is staring at me from his place at the table, shaking his head.

"What is with you?" he asks.

NOT NOW, I tell my tears. "I'm having a bad day," I tell him.

"What's up?"

"Nothing. Just a bad mood. I'm fine."

I go back to my room. It's only early afternoon and my brain's already exploding from all the crap that equals today. Sometimes everything seems to hit the fan at once. That's just how life is sometimes, I guess. I can't remember a worse day since that one in seventh grade when 1) A.J. Summers dumped me for JoAnne Pearlman, 2) a wasp stung me during lunch period, and 3) I got gum stuck in my hair and had to cut four inches off to get it out. Only this time it's way worse. I think I'm off my rocker, my best friend hates me, and there might be a murderer running around town I have to worry about.

It's like that book I had when I was a kid, times a thousand: Arielle's Terrible, Horrible, No Good, Very Bad Day.

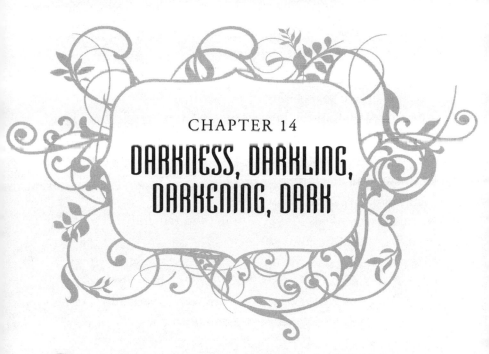

CHAPTER 14
DARKNESS, DARKLING, DARKENING, DARK

CASEY'S BOBBED HER HAIR and wears knee-high boots over her jeans now. Her clothes are black, not pink. And when I hug her she smells like musty perfume.

"You look different," I say as I pull away.

She pinches my arm. "You look exactly the same."

"Yeah, well, what can I say."

"Yeah, well, at least I didn't come home to find you with bleached hair and a fake tan," she answers, winking at me.

I help the fam bring Casey's ten thousand bags inside the apartment. Dad is wearing an apron that says *NO COFFEE NO WORKEE.*

"It's cozy here." Casey looks around the room at the shelves, Mom's desk squeezed in the corner, the closet-sized dining room with the whiteboard on the wall that says, "CASEY COMING HOME TODAY!!!!"

"We told you we downsized," Mom says.

"It's weird, it still feels like home," she says.

"Of course it's home," Dad says. "Especially when you're here!"

They hug. He kisses her cheek.

"Isn't her hair just *perfect*?" Mom asks.

"You had it short like that when you were a little girl," Dad says, all dreamy.

Not to be a spoilsport, but I find their pride in her mere *haircut* slightly disgusting.

"Where's my stuff?" Casey asks.

"In the closet right there." I point and remember the binder. I don't say anything, though.

"I'm going to ship them to Cambridge," she says. "Sorry, I didn't realize they took up an entire closet here."

"Oh, it's fine," Mom says, beaming as she clears her magazines and Dad's crossword puzzle books off the table.

Chloe and I haven't even talked since the fight about Brody. It's been a week. I miss her so much I could scream.

Lunches alone feel pathetic. I avoid the people-happy quad and spend Monday alone near the bleachers on the football field. Scarfing my pizza slice, I see Tex coming out of the Mechanics building—a garage sprawling with guys in coveralls—and wave him over.

"I didn't know you sat here." He slings his backpack and motorcycle helmet onto the bench next to me and sits close. I put my hand on his knee.

"I usually don't." I wipe my mouth with a napkin and wish I had a mint to erase my pepperoni breath. "What are you doing over here?"

"I have Mechanics fourth period. I usually stay late."

"Ah."

I smile at him and lean in for a kiss—instinct—but he stiffens and sucks air in his nose.

It's not a good response. It's not the drop-everything-and-embrace-me-like-there's-no-tomorrow reaction I'd expected. And it's like someone pours hot water all over me. I can feel my neck redden, my cheeks flush.

I'm stunned.

"Don't think I don't want this," he says. "But . . . Arielle, I don't think we should keep doing this. You don't need someone like me in your life. I wouldn't wish me on anyone."

"Let me make that decision," I say, offended.

He looks at my hand on his knee. He puts his hand on my hand, and even that—even the simple warmth of his palm—melts me with a tiny bit of hope.

"You can't make that decision," he says, "because you don't really know me that well. There's so much you don't know."

"So let me."

He shakes his head. "Really. It's . . . this is different."

"You can trust me."

"Some things you never tell anyone. You never talk about them."

I'm frantic inside—how do I stop this? What have I done? "Nothing will change what I think of you," I say. "Did someone hurt you?"

"It doesn't matter what you say," he says, his expression never changing. "Please don't try to get me to tell you when I don't want to."

A long silence hangs there between us. I stare at our hands again.

"You can tell me anything and I'll still care about you," I say softly.

He closes his eyes. He doesn't even flinch at the word *care*.

Our hands are still there, on his knee.

I can't help but wonder what could be that terrible. Was he molested? Was he a klepto, a pyro? An animal-torturer? Did he hurt someone?

And of course . . . does all of this have something to do with his sister? I put a finger to my wrist and can feel the mad, mad rhythm ticking in my vein.

"What I did," he says. "It's unforgiveable."

"What is it?"

He just shakes his head.

"Please, Tex, what is it? Did someone hurt you?"

He makes a *pffft* sound. "No."

"Did you hurt someone?"

"Maybe."

There's a pounding in my ears. An *oh no* drop in my stomach. I hope, hope, hope I'm wrong. Please be wrong.

But he doesn't give me the chance to ask. He watches our hands on his knee. And then he takes his out from under mine and makes some dumb excuse before leaving me here on the bleachers alone.

Sleep's a complete joke tonight. I awaken with jerks, I swear, a dozen times. I have a dream that Perdita is living in the room next to me (I'm in my old house), and she's my sister, and she doesn't believe me when I tell her she's dead. And when I wake around four A.M. and enter the hall to go to the bathroom, a weird tree-looking shape bleeds out of the left side of my vision and I get a rolling feeling that starts in my mouth and then takes over my head. The déjà vu's so strong I have to grip the doorframe. All I can think is, this happened before! This happened before!

After some seconds pass, the tree is long gone, and I can't remember what it is that happened.

Back in bed, I'm convinced I just sleepwalked for the first time. And when the morning comes, I tell myself it was maybe even a dream.

But a part of me knows it was like all those other befores.

There's nothing left on my fingernails to bite. I really don't feel well.

After school the next day, I get off the bus early in my old neighborhood and walk past the Dells'. I lie and tell myself I just want to walk the long way home. When I stand outside his house for a moment, I imagine ringing the doorbell and try to think of what I'd say to Tex. But as I stare at their door from the sidewalk, I just feel overwhelmingly tiny and pathetic. I don't have the guts to knock.

In the gold late-afternoon haze, an airplane cuts through the sky and I hug my arms. Even though it's still sunny (it's pretty sunny every day of the year here), it's starting to get colder. Then I hear a snipping noise and look ahead, over the hedges that separate the neighbor's yard from the Dells'. I see that gardening hat bobbing up and down and I gasp a little gasp, remembering the creepy Judge. At that moment, the head rises fully over the hedge—great, the last person I feel like interacting with right now, Mr. Peeping Tom himself—but then I realize it's a woman. She's probably in her forties, blond-gray, and gives me a gap-toothed smile and a wave.

"Hello," she says.

"Hi," I say, a little shocked. For starters, I was expecting the creepoid and not her when I saw the hat. Secondly, is this friendly-looking woman *married* to him? God, if only she knew her husband spied on teenage girls and stared at them like a pedo! "You live there?"

"Oh, I'm Riley's daughter," she says. "I take care of the place when he's in Costa Rica. Just his roses, mainly."

I don't know what to say—she's staring at me with the eager face of someone who wants to keep chatting. "He's on vacation in Costa Rica?" I ask after a moment.

"Yeah, he's out of the country nine months out of the year now—and he refuses to pay for a gardener." She laughs and shakes her head.

"Huh." I stare at her, thinking, I'm so glad my dad's not a total creep.

"His last trip, he was gone June to September," she says. "And then he came back and started talking about getting a puppy. I was like, 'Dad, roses are one thing—but I am *not* taking responsibility for a puppy for months at a time.'"

I laugh awkwardly. "Totally. Well . . . have a nice day."

"You too!" she waves with her shears.

I practically jog away, and when I get to the intersection of his street and my old street, I keep on. I don't know which I'm more scared to see right now—the house I grew up in that I can't enter anymore, or the lake where I saw Perdita's body. On my way home, I keep thinking about that woman trimming the roses. What that must be like, to have a total creeper for a dad. Then her words echo, and I realize something.

June to September.

The Judge was in Costa Rica the month she died. So there's no way he killed Perdita.

Tonight's the show: in a few hours I'm going to be onstage, belting out my lines in front of a crowd of familiar strangers. But I can't concentrate on my lines and instead I turn on my computer and watch TV. I pick a random show called *Real Life Mysteries*, with a cheesy, computer-animated opening and a Casio keyboard song. I'm expecting aliens and ghosts, Sasquatch and mermaids, but instead it turns out to be about mental illness. If I wanted to watch some show about disorders, I'd just go knock on my mom the therapist's door and ask her how her day went.

But I don't turn it off yet, because it's about a little schizophrenic girl with a halo-frizz of gold hair, and when she's introduced to the camera, she says, "I see ghosts in all the mirrors."

I sit up straighter in my bed and turn the volume up. I get especially bothered when I see the little girl throw a tantrum that reminds me of someone possessed. She contorts her face, shudders and jolts, opens her strawberry lips in silent scream. The doctor in the lab coat explains that she's got "sensory overload" from her hallucinations.

Why did I choose to watch this? When I close the computer window and make the show go away, I notice my hand is shaking. I look up at my reflection hanging above my dresser, my hair a tangled aura, my eyes glossy-wide with fear.

I see ghosts in all the mirrors.

The sight of that tantrum chilled my bones. And I know why. I open the video on my desktop—six and a half hours long—and I skip through it again to watch myself spasm and tremor and topple off my bed.

"No," I whisper.

It's ugly. It fits.

I realize what I look like in that video. I look like this woman I saw once in a mental hospital on Take Your Daughter to Work Day. I went to work with my mom when I was twelve and I still remember seeing this woman strapped to a bed, spitting and screaming and trying to break free. It was so disturbing.

"What's *wrong* with her?" I asked my mom after we passed the room.

"She's psychotic," my mom answered, all breezy, as if she was saying something as blah as "she's blond."

Psychotic.

What if all this time, I've been convinced I'm seeing ghosts—but really I'm just crazy?

Something's *wrong* with me.

Not special, as in, oh, I have a gift! I can see ghosts! But *wrong*, as in neurotransmitters are misfiring or bad brain chemicals.

I Google "schizophrenia symptoms."

And I'm aware this is physically impossible, but I swear my pulse disappears as my eyes drink in the words.

Hallucinations.

Delusions.

Disorganized behavior.

Trouble focusing.

Poor school performance.

Often begins in teen years.

"No, no, no," I say, hands flying up to tear at my cheeks, as if I could remove my own face like a mask.

Going to perform a monologue in front of a hundred of your high school colleagues and their parents is pretty much the last thing you'd be in the mood for if you were also worrying about your sanity.

I just can't wait 'til it's over. Everyone's got fluorescent programs in their hands and plastic cups of Kool-Aid. Pierre's walking around, schmoozing. The voices on top of voices echo in the hall, eerie and overlapping, toneless music.

There's Chloe's mom, Trixie, and her boyfriend pointing at the bulletin board. I wonder where Chloe is. My parents immediately see them and go over to say hi. I stay with Casey, who's standing and staring at Tex's parents, who are around the corner sitting on a planter.

"It's the Dells," she says quietly. "I should go say hi to them."

"Go ahead."

"I wonder why they're here?"

"Tex is in this class."

"Oh, yeah. He transferred. That's right." She lines her toes up perfectly, stares at her boots. "I feel so bad for them. It makes me so sad I want to cry."

"I know. Did you hear about what the paper said?"

"What paper?"

"About how they found DNA under Perdita's fingernails," I whisper. "And now they're saying 'foul play.'"

I've never seen a human being go white in a breath's time until right now.

"'They,' like, the police?"

"I guess."

She doesn't say anything for a minute. "I'm going to be sick. I can't talk about this."

"Sorry," I say. "I thought you already knew."

"I need to find the bathroom," she says, and leaves me there alone, staring at the mingling crowds of parents and the little kids running around with Kool-Aid lips.

I'm up third. Third! I have no idea what the first one was like because, although I watched it from the side of the stage, here, I was somewhere else. Somewhere in a quiet, terrible world of dread. I wander past the seats and dim lighting and go backstage. Chloe's in the corner penning her eyeliner in the mirror. Tex is back here, too, spinning on an office chair all alone and mouthing his lines to the wall.

Don't think about your best friend who's no longer your best friend.

Don't think about the boy you want so bad who had to drop such a vague, sickening bombshell and then ignore you like a germ.

Don't think about how you're schizo, your brain's rotten with disorder, and sooner or later you'll have to meet a doctor and spill the beans and the pretending will be over.

Face the stage; face reality.

When the second monologue is done I take a breath. I'd rather melt and sob but I walk onstage instead. The room is hushed and dark; people's faces are shadows; the spotlight I'm standing in, blinding.

I stand there, waiting for a second.

There's something . . . building. In me. Not good.

Stop it, I tell the roller coaster in my belly.

"Oh, Mama," I say to the audience. "Just look at me one minute as though you really saw me." I swallow. "Mama, fourteen years have gone by." I swallow. My voice seems to shrink. "I'm dead."

I freeze, eyes on the blaring yolky lights, swallow again.

I swallow again. I swallow again.

Swallowswallowswallow.

It's happening. I'm about to hallucinate.

"Don't look," I hear myself saying. Louder, louder. "Don't look."

Don't turn your head, Arielle. Don't! Don't look to the left! Don't do it!

That thing, though, at the side of my vision, it's begging to be looked at.

I can't stop, ugh, I'm a magnet, I must, I'm turning, I'm looking left and . . .

WHAM.

I see . . . I see *myself* . . . like I'm removed from myself. I see myself with a neck so long, stretched uuuuuuup, like pictures in my *Alice in Wonderland* book only it's me, wide-eyed, and—

All at once, wow. Oh.

I'm nothing but a feeling.

The roller coaster is serious. Skin tingles, screams. Hear it? That sweet ringing in my ears, watery music, little sugar voices, eeeee, aaaaaa, tickling me, making me want to laugh, cry out, slip, scream, walls hugging me like arms and bright lights and I know, with a sudden flood of bliss, that wait! Waitwaitwait.

This has all happened before. Let me tell you! Let me tell you all about it! I am bigger than everything; I am smaller than nothing. THIS is the THIS that has already happened. THIS IS WHAT HAS BEEN ON THE TIP OF MY TONGUE! The roller coaster in my stomach rises so high that it pushes me down into blackness, blankness. Swallow it. Swallow it. Fall. The floor is coming, the floor is coming, darkness, darkling, darkening, dark.

CHAPTER 15

I SURVIVED

I HEAR THUNDER ROLLING beneath me, wheels.

Swishing noises bloom into voices.

Finally, blurry heads bob around me but I don't know who they are. Their lips are moving and I hear words but I don't know. My body hurts. My head screams. Colors change. Who is the president? What year is it? What is my name?

I close my eyes again.

A purple curtain. I'm thirsty and I look around. Mom sits on a chair, looking at me with no reading glasses. Her eyes are red and her makeup is runny and she doesn't seem to care.

"There you are," she says.

After the jelly on my temples and the electrodes on my skull, after the horrible, tapping, weird, shut-eyed darkness of the MRI tunnel, after being poked with needles, peeing in cups, and answering every medical question under the sun, the doctor tells me I have a condition called temporal lobe epilepsy and it caused a seizure.

"You were lucky—some woman in the front row who was a nurse knew what was happening, cushioned your head, and turned you on your side so you wouldn't choke. You bit your tongue up pretty bad," she says. "Have you ever had this happen before?"

The doctor must be making a mistake. It was one seizure!

"Ever woken up in the morning sore, or with a bitten tongue, anything like that?"

I shake my head. But then I remember falling off my bed—and the time my lamp was broken. She asks if I ever have feelings of déjà vu, or like everything is unfamiliar. If I ever stare into space, or say weird things I don't recall later. Strange smells or tastes. Moving of my lips, swallowing, repeating movements with my hands without realizing.

She tells me about the medication I'm going to start taking, warning me about side effects. I'm just shocked. I thought I was loony tunes, not brain-damaged.

"It's not brain damage," she says.

Apparently I have a lot to learn about epilepsy.

Dr. Brewster describes these other seizures called simple partials and complex partials. She says it can be as simple as spacing out for a few seconds or getting a wave of déjà vu. She tells me my repetitive swallowing is a symptom of these complex partial seizures, and my "feeling like I've felt a feeling before" is part of it, too. She says my seizures sometimes spread to the occipital lobe of my brain, so sometimes the feeling becomes a hallucination—the times when I feel like something's on the tip of my tongue, or I just forgot something, or I know something but can't put it into words.

I'm not crazy. There's a reason for it all.

Life suddenly makes sense.

So. Completely. Overwhelming.

Dr. Brewster recommends I join an online support group to meet other people who *share my condition.*

It's so weird to just wake up one day in a hospital, being told you have a condition, knowing your whole life has to do a one-eighty because you're not who you thought you were. When she leaves the room to talk to my family about my diagnosis, my meds, and what to do if I have another seizure, I cry harder than I've cried in years. I don't even know if they're tears of joy or fear or sadness. Pretty sure the answer is all of the above.

When I get home, I sit in my room, take the orange prescription bottles out of the brown paper bag from the pharmacy, and line them up on my dresser. This change rocked everything. It didn't ask my permission. It didn't factor in what I wanted. That's life, Arielle. It's a lesson never over. It's the way it is and there's no squirming out of it.

I have an answer now. A diagnosis posing as an answer, anyway—but it only seems to fling the door open to an endless march of questions. When did this begin? As a kid? Is that why I imagined the dead circled around the living? Was the faint chill I felt sometimes after Justin died—was that just a disease, and not his spirit? When I spoke to the air alone and swore he heard me, when I saw a pale glint in a window I thought was Perdita, was it all lies, a brain trick a pill can kill?

Are there really no such things as ghosts?

I know what the doctor said. I know all about epilepsy's laundry list of symptoms. But nothing I've read, and nothing anyone's said, has mentioned actually seeing straight-up ghosts. A feeling of déjà vu? Totally. A weird pattern over your vision?

Yeah, I read about a lady who saw that. But *ghosts*, actual ghosts with holes for eyes sitting in your room and looking at you—the ghost of a girl you know in a window—that stuff is more than epilepsy. Isn't it?

"I still believe," I whisper, staring at the air, which holds so much more than it appears.

I pick up the orange prescription bottle, shake it, and hear the rattle of pills.

Casey hugs me so hard it hurts and says how traumatizing it was. Dad tells me that was the scariest moment of his life and he doesn't know what he would do without me. Mom cries unabashedly now, which is so out of character for her. The last time I saw her cry this hard was the day we sprinkled Justin in the sea.

I rest my head on her shoulder and she says that all you can do sometimes is try to do better.

"I, for one, am going to stop harping on you about your grades," Mom says.

Apparently a lot of teenagers with epilepsy have a hard time concentrating in school, so she says she's not going to be so strict with me about grades and homework anymore. I'd fist pump, but I'm not in the mood.

"I'm going to try to come home more," Casey says. "All this has made me realize just how important it is to spend time together."

"You never know," Dad says, shaking his head. "You just never know."

"How are you?" Mom asks me. "You brave, wonderful girl?"

I stare at the window, where outside the dark, faraway tree-tops do a little dance in the light of the streetlamp. I still can't figure out how I feel about anything. Maybe I liked it better the way it was before, even if I was driving myself crazy thinking I was crazy. That question seems so much deeper than what I know my mom means—how am I? How *am* I?

"I don't know," I tell them. "But I'm here."

Chloe comes over early the next morning. I try not to show her how much it means to me when she shuts my bedroom door, steps into my room, and plunks next to me on my bed, circling her too-tan, too-thin arms around me, not talking for a long time. When she pulls away, there's red all around the brown irises of her eyes.

"I was so worried," she says.

I laugh nervously.

"Really, Arielle. It was like—my life flashed before my eyes."

"*I* was the one who had the seizure."

"I know. But I was filled with this terror, and—and I just thought, 'What if you never get to talk to her again? What if you never, ever get to hang out with your best friend in the whole universe again, and the last time you ever saw her, you were fighting over a stupid boy?'"

Her tears are spilling right now. Another love-it-or-hate-it feature of BFF-hood is that tears are a hundred percent contagious. So I start welling up, too.

"Seriously," she says. "I wanted to hurt myself, thinking that. You are so important to me. You're my best friend."

"It's okay," I say.

"I missed you; you have to know that," she says. "I was just being a stubborn bee-atch."

Some invisible muscle somewhere relaxes in me, a loosening of anxiety that's been there since Chloe and I fought weeks ago.

"Tex messaged me on Facebook and asked for your address," Chloe says. "I think he wants to send flowers or something."

"That's really sweet," I say, drawing my legs up and hugging them.

"Can I ask a question about epilepsy?" Chloe asks.

"Fire away."

"Is that why we were fighting and why you seemed so . . . far away?"

I stare at Chloe, at her blow-dried blond locks, her made-to-be-a-model cheekbones. Even though she's right here, I miss her. I can't explain it; I just miss her while she's within inches, I do.

I could tell her the truth. Before, there was no option: it was only truth with us. But if I tell her I just don't like Brody and I think she should ditch him, if I say the seizure and epilepsy don't seem to have anything to do with the fact I've felt a little messed up since Perdita died—maybe it was seeing the body, I don't know, but I'm just haunted by the whole thing and even the meds they've started me on haven't changed that—if I say, I saw a threat in a dead girl's drawer. And I am totally butt-crazy over her brother who hinted that he might have killed her. And even though I know epilepsy explains a few things, I don't care what the doctors say. I still believe in ghosts. If I say the truth, I don't think I'll have a friend. And I need Chloe. I don't want to lose her, but there are certain things I just have to accept she won't understand, and how could she when I don't quite, either?

"Possibly," is all I say.

She nods, satisfied.

It was a compromise. I didn't lie; I didn't tell the truth.

Tex does *not* send flowers.

He brings them to me in person.

It's hours after Chloe and I make up, late morning. I'm watching some TV show about people who disappeared and were never found, and, hi, I'm a textbook slob: unbrushed hair, a T-shirt with holes in it, sweatpants.

I don't recognize the *knock-knock-KNOCK* but figure it's Casey.

"Come in," I say.

And suddenly, in a blink, Tex is there, closing my bedroom door behind him. Jean jacket. Hair falling onto his perfect cheeks. Lilies in one hand and car keys in another. My room with bras and panties scattered on the floor. My room that probably smells like I should open a window. My room with me in it, looking like some homeless person. My slippers don't even match! Freud on one foot and a bunny on the other.

"Chloe gave me the address," he says.

I stand up. "Oh, cool."

"I wanted to surprise you. That's why I didn't call."

"Well, it worked; I'm surprised."

I rest my hand on my cheek, hoping to cover about half my face with this casual gesture.

"Can I sit?" he asks.

"Sure."

Kill me. The boy whose babies I want to make is stepping over a pile of my dirty clothes to sit beside me on my bed.

"I would've cleaned if I knew you were coming," I say. "This is embarrassing."

"It's not that bad," he says.

Our legs are touching. My sweatpants to his black jeans.

"Yes it is," I say.

I stare at my orange prescription bottles, wishing I could sweep them into the dresser drawer.

"Plus, I look ugly," I say. "Don't look at me."

"Arielle," he says seriously, leaning over his knee and into me a little, staring at me hard with quivering eyes. "I don't give a shit about any of that. You're not ugly. Even in sweatpants, you're hotter than any other girl I know."

I roll my eyes.

"I was so worried about you," he says.

"Yeah, I know, everyone was worried," I say. "I'm okay."

"I don't think you get it," he says. "I feel like I have an ulcer or something."

He does look in pain, and he clutches his gut for a second as if to show me he's being real.

"Because of me?"

"Because I've been so *worried*," he says.

"It's just epilepsy," I say. "It's pretty common, actually."

"It's more than the seizure," he says. "I've been worried every second with you. Afraid of saying the wrong thing. I get an inch closer to you, I'm worried I'll lose you. I see more of you, I worry about how empty that time's going to feel when you go away."

I feel my brow wrinkle in the opposite of understanding.

"I've been worried like that for months," he goes on. "Like, I can't eat; I can't sleep. Nothing's the way it was. I'm . . . losing it sometimes."

"'It' what?"

He taps his temple. "My mind."

It's like a hand clasps over a secret part of me. Those are *my* words. That's *my* truth. *I've* been the one losing my mind.

"*You* were the one who pushed *me* away," I say—and then I remember the reason. The nameless *thing* he did.

Oh, the cloud. The cloud that passes over me, over this room, cooling his thigh pressed against my thigh in our side-by-side position.

"What I did was terrible," he says.

It shadows everything and I don't want him to keep talking. Please, please don't say what I think you're going to say . . .

"I stalked my sister," he says. He watches the air when he says it, doesn't even turn to me. I have to remind myself, now is the furthest from what would be considered an appropriate time to analyze what perfection the shape of his profile is.

"Stalked her?" My pulse goes from sixty to a hundred-sixty in a damp-sick second.

"Online," he says.

"But she *lived* with you—"

"I did it to torture her." He doesn't move. "I don't know. I made up this Facebook account. . . . I said terrible things, posted fucked-up pictures on her page. She was so scared after that she deleted her account."

Oh! OH! I suck air in, realizing. "That was *you*?"

"You know . . . you knew about that?" he asks, turning to me.

"Well, Casey said something about it. And Raffi."

"What'd they tell you?"

"Just that . . . someone was stalking her online."

He turns back to the air again. "Yeah, when the cops came to take her report I sat in my room, erasing every trace of what I'd done. They never found out it was me."

"Why did you *do* that?" I ask.

"I was mad at her," he says. "She stole a guitar of mine and pawned it. She ratted on me for smoking weed to a teacher at my old school—a family friend—told them I was a 'loadie.' I'm pretty sure that's why they didn't renew my scholarship."

He stops talking, shakes his head, and sighs. "None of it matters now. Not any of it."

I wait for him to go on, expecting the news to get worse, the story to go further.

"And then . . ." I gulp. "What happened?"

"And then she died."

The silence is thick and pain-filled.

"How."

"I know what the article said, but I still can't shake the idea that she did it to herself," he says. "And I drove her to it with that stupid Facebook shit."

This relief I feel sings inside me, and I know how weird it is, but I can't help it. Hallelujah!

He didn't kill her. No way.

"Tex," I say softly. "You didn't have anything to do with her death. And it really looks like it wasn't suicide. The police have evidence."

He blows out a long breath, closes his eyes, and his body slumps a little with relaxation. "It feels so good to hear that," he says. "Sooooo good. You don't even know."

I rub his back, softly, in a little circle.

"That was your secret?"

"Yes."

"There's nothing else?"

"That's it."

"Why was it so hard to tell me that?"

"I didn't want you to hate me," he says. "Think I was a creep or something."

"I don't hate you."

Our knees are touching and he interlaces his fingers with mine and we talk. Or more like, I talk—about the epilepsy diagnosis and how I'm afraid my pills are going to zombify my brain, about Chloe and her horrible boyfriend. And you know what? Saying these things, having someone to hold me and tell me it's going to be all right and that I'm wonderful, I'm strong, I'm brave, and I will survive all this—it's even better than making out with the hottest boy in Velero.

"How are you so *nice*?" I ask him, flicking tears from my eye corners and staring at him in amazement. "Like, where did you come from?"

"That's exactly how I felt about you," he says. "When you came and sat next to me at Perdita's wake. And when you talked to me in Theater, and acted like you cared, like you really cared what happened to me."

I rest my head on his shoulder.

"Sometimes I think about all the terrible shit that's happened," he says. "Getting kicked out of my old school. Perdita. But I wouldn't have you if it weren't for those things. I don't know. I guess good things can come out of the bad. They can't be separated."

I look at our hands meshed together, his tan, long fingers and my short, white ones. "No, they can't."

"So what's your secret?" he asks. "A while back you said you had one."

"Oh yeah," I say, a hot, subtle panic creeping under my skin. "So I did."

"I told you mine. I'm sure it can't be worse than that."

Gulp.

You wanna bet, Tex?

"I've felt crazy lately," I say, and I know I'm not going to stop. I look away so I don't have to see his reaction as the words leak from my lips. "Since the end of summer. I don't think you know, but I saw your sister's body being pulled from the lake. The cops zipped her up in a body bag, and even the sound of the zipper has, like, haunted me. I started seeing things in my room sometimes—weird things—mostly this skeleton girl and

I wondered if it was her—the doctors say the hallucinations were because of my epilepsy. But everything with your sister, like always thinking about her, bothered by what happened to her—obsessing, dreaming about her . . . it just doesn't stop."

I squeeze my eyes shut for this part. "It's like her ghost is haunting me. My brain just goes there all the time. Who killed her? Who killed her? I still have moments where I swear she's . . . she's around. Her spirit is still around. I've seen her. I've heard her. I mean, I know I'm epileptic, but . . . I still think it doesn't explain everything." I swallow. "Tex, you're going to hate me when I tell you this. But I opened her drawer and snooped through her things when I was changing out of her bathing suit in her room that day I was over."

I can't keep my eyes shut forever. I open them, and see him staring at me in disbelief, cloudy-eyed and furrow-browed.

"I'm sorry," I say.

"What did you see?" he asks.

"Just . . . I mean, I just looked at a couple things. I saw a Tampax box with money in it. I picked up this heart-shaped box, and that's when—you'll think I'm nuts, but—I heard her voice. She said to look at the bottom. There was a secret compartment, and a letter inside."

"You're kidding."

I shake my head. "And the letter has been *hounding* me. It was written in red pen and it said—" I close my eyes and remember it like a photograph. "'Bitch, if you don't give me what I asked for your life as you know it is over.'"

"Whoa," he says. He seems to not even care about how creepy I am. He's just intrigued by the detail.

"You should show it to me," he says. "That could be, like, evidence. I mean, really. That could be important."

"You don't think I'm crazy for thinking I saw her ghost?"

"I believe in ghosts," he says simply.

I stare at his lips in amazement.

"I totally believe in ghosts," he says, even firmer. "Since she died, I get a chilly feeling every time I open her door. And the *dreams* I've had."

"You dream about her?"

"All the fucking time. And sometimes, late at night—I swear I hear knocking, a quiet knocking, in the wall between our rooms. It never scared me. I just figured—I mean, it's common knowledge, right? So many people see ghosts. It's not crazy at all."

Comfort blooms from toes to fingertips. Not just because Tex doesn't think I'm out of my skull, but because he actually believes in ghosts, too—that people's spirits probably *do* live on in other forms and I'm not the only one who thinks so.

"You're not mad at me?" I ask.

"What right do I have to be mad at you?" he asks. "Plus, you think you're the only one who's been obsessed with my sister since she died? Look around, I'll bet you half the town is looking over their shoulder, avoiding that lake, having nightmares about her. We all want to know what happened to her. In fact—can you show the letter to me? I want to see it. I mean, maybe we should call the police."

"Okay . . ." I say. "Now?"

"Why not?" he says. "You busy?"

I laugh, looking down at my sweatpants. "Um . . . do I look busy?"

"All right," he says. We're so close he can probably see my pores. "But before everything gets weird . . . before we go into Perdita's room and start looking for things, I want to kiss you again. Is that still allowed?"

Does he really need to ask?

"It's allowed," I tell him. "I can't believe you still want to—"

He shuts me up in the best way you can imagine, his lips on mine, his hands in my tangled hair, his body pinning mine to the bed. I've never known such a perfect kisser—a mix of sweetness with just the right amount of push. He pulls away and runs his thumb along my chin. His lips kissed pink.

We go over the freeway overpass, circle around the supermarket and movie theater, and cut over to my old street. I actually gasp when I see what the new neighbors did to the house I grew up in—they cut down the tree outside and painted the whole place blue.

"You okay?" Tex asks.

"My house . . ." I say, finger to lips.

"Yeah?"

I drop my fingers. "My old house," is all I can say.

I look ahead and a heave settles heavy in my middle. The sadness morphs into acceptance. I fight the urge to look over my shoulder, or to ask him to make a U-turn so I can stare up at my old window and wonder who lives there now.

A minute later, Tex parks in his driveway and we hop out of the car. I follow him inside.

"Hey, Mom," Tex says.

His mom sits at the dining room table, flipping through a magazine. She's got her frosted hair up in a high ponytail and wears workout clothes and sneakers, which makes her look young. Whenever I've seen her in the past she's been in a blazer and skirt—or, at the funeral, in black. When she sees me, she puts the magazine down and smiles.

"Hi, Arielle!" she says. "How *are* you?"

At first I think the enthusiastic response is her remembering me from the barbeque both our families went to, or the fact

I'm Casey's sister. But then I realize she was there when I had my seizure in front of half the world. And that enthusiasm is concern.

"I'm doing better," I say.

"Good," she says.

I stand awkwardly, not knowing what to say next.

"How are *you*?" I ask.

She takes in a deep breath. "Surviving." She smiles with her mouth but not her eyes. "Is Casey in town for Thanksgiving?"

"Yeah."

"What are you guys going to do?"

"You know, turkey, stuffing, the usual."

"That's great. Tell Casey I say hi."

"Come on," Tex murmurs, pulling my sleeve. "We're going upstairs," he tells his mom.

"See you two later," she says.

The playful way she says it makes me wonder—what has Tex said about me? Do his parents know about us? Not that we're an "us" or anything.

Are we?

"Okay, let's get this over with."

I move out of the way and he opens the door. My ecstasy cools to nerves as I remember that we're here not to make out, but to gather info on his dead sister.

Whoosh, the rainbow colors and faint musty sweetness of Perdita's room smack me with déjà vu. The hurricane of clothes on the floor. The bed that still has her impression in it. Her vanity. I touch a pair of sunglasses and shrink my finger away, afraid to disturb anything. I stare at the pictures around the doorway and mirror again, mostly people I've never seen. I wait for flowers to grow out of their eyes and mouths like last time, but the pictures just stay pictures. I know I'm supposed to be relieved—thanks, meds! But a part of me pangs. My window to that special world—where spirits flare and mystery outspreads—is lost.

I miss flowers growing out of mouths in photographs.

I miss the certainty of whispering ghosts.

But there Tex stands, staring at the vanity, me beside him. And even though this is so not the time and/or place, our dusty reflection makes me think: we do make a pretty couple.

Okay, Arielle. Focus.

"It's in here," I say, pointing to the drawer.

"You can open it," he says. "What are you afraid of?"

I shrug and pull it open. I grab the heart-shaped paper mache box.

"It's in here," I say.

I pull the bottom off.

"Secret compartment," I say.

"No wonder the cops didn't see it when they searched her room," he says. "I wondered."

"They searched her room?"

"Yeah, but they weren't in there super long. At that point I think everyone thought it was an accident. I think they were just making sure she hadn't left a suicide note."

I hold the upside-down box up, show him the folded paper. "Read it."

He picks it up and I can see the red pen bleeding through. I look over his shoulder at the bright, smudgy lettering.

BITCH IF YOU DON'T GIVE ME WHAT I ASKED FOR YOUR LIFE AS YOU KNOW IT IS OVER

I actually shiver when I read it again. Those ugly, crude, crimson letters remind me of blood.

"Whoever wrote this obviously wanted to hurt her," I say.

"Arielle." He looks at it closer. "Perdita totally wrote this."

What?

Come again?

"No . . ." I say.

"Yes. She wrote notes in red pen all the time, lipstick some-times. Classic Perdita. And I know her handwriting."

"Well . . ." I stare at it again, the letters suddenly seeming not scary at all with this new information. I'm so confused. "Why would she write that?"

"I don't know." He folds it back up and puts it in her drawer. "Where's the money you said she had?"

"Here." I grab the Tampax box and hand it to him.

"Whoa," he says as he grabs the bills. They're all twenties. The stack is huge, much bigger than I'd guessed. I watch him count them, mouthing the numbers, and I fight the urge to interrupt him with a kiss.

"Jesus, Arielle—there's almost two thousand dollars in here," he says.

"Wow."

"Where the hell did she get this?" he asks. "She never had a job."

"*I* don't know."

"Maybe she stole it," Tex says, putting the money back in the box.

"No."

"You didn't know Perdita," he says. "She wasn't an angel. She got kicked out of Rite Aid in tenth grade for stealing nail polish."

"Yeah, this isn't a bottle of *Wet n Wild*," I say. "This is a couple thousand dollars."

"She got in trouble for joyriding last year," he says.

"Whose car?" I ask, surprised.

He shrugs. "Some guy who left his keys in it. She stole a credit card from my dad's wallet, too, ran up a crazy bill shoe shopping and lied about it to his face."

He puts the box back in the drawer and closes it.

"I don't know," he says. "I feel weird in here. I don't want my mom to know we're doing this—she'd flip her lid. She wants to keep this place exactly how it was when Perdita 'left it.'" Then he does the "crazy" motion with a finger circling an ear.

As we close the door behind us, I'm thick with disappointment.

I thought I had an answer, a clue belonging to a murderer.

But all it was was a nothing-note.

I've had enough of doctors for a while, but Mom ignores my whining and drives me to my follow-up appointment that afternoon anyway, saying nothing in the car. I know she's pre-occupied because she lets a whole heavy metal song play on the radio without changing the station. She's had that lip-biting, worry-wrinkled look on her face ever since I seized onstage. I want to yell at her, *I'm still here! I'm taking my pills and I'll be all right!* But instead, I stare out the window at the chop-chop-chop of trees, buildings, power lines.

Apparently the doctor just has to check on me to make sure I haven't had another seizure or a nasty reaction to the meds. Dr. Brewster is ponytailed and so young-looking it seems mathematically impossible she can be a doctor, but the lab coat and stethoscope-thing dangling around her neck convince me. After a quick Q and A—I'm fine, I'm fine, I'm fine—she asks if there are any more questions we have for her.

"Nope," I say, at the same time as my mom says, "Just one."

Dr. Brewster and I look at my mom, who is strangling her purse with her hands.

"My son died," she says in this rigid, rehearsed voice. "About ten years ago. He drowned at summer camp."

She waits, and Dr. Brewster says the obligatory "I'm so sorry to hear that."

"Thank you," Mom continues. "He was a good swimmer. He'd had lessons. I always wondered how it happened. Now that I've learned about Arielle, I wonder . . . if he was epileptic, too."

Dr. Brewster sits back down on her chair. "Well, there's really no way to know for sure."

"He fell out of bed several times," Mom says, voice shaking. "And his sixth-grade teacher tried to tell us he went into 'trances.' I never thought to have him tested."

I never knew any of this. I'm a human lump; I can't even move.

"It's been *hounding* me, for years, this question of why," she goes on. "Why would that happen for no reason? And I feel so guilty thinking there *was* a reason, and it was staring us in the face—and we didn't catch it."

Rivers now. Mom's frantically trying to stop them, but they're outrunning her fingers.

Dr. Brewster's expression is a mirror of pain. She pulls her chair closer, and reaches out and touches my mom's knee. "It's possible that's why," she says. "I've known some families that have more than one sibling with epilepsy."

"My aunt had it," my mom says. "And I think a cousin on her side had it, too. I just didn't even think to have him tested—I could have saved his life—"

Dr. Brewster hands Mom a tissue and lets her blow her nose. "Listen to me," she says. "There was nothing you could have done."

Mom starts crying so hard I have to look away. I have to close my eyes.

"You couldn't know," Dr. Brewster says again.

"But—"

"This was not your fault," Dr. Brewster interrupts.

I open my eyes and watch my mom's trembling hand with the balled-up tissue. Her eyes stop watering, and she stares into the air like she sees something new, something that wasn't there before.

"This. Was. Not. Your. Fault," Dr. Brewster says again.

The words echo against the flat white walls and linoleum tiles. The words grow wings and fly.

Mom lets out the longest breath. "I feel like I've waited years for someone to tell me that," she says, before taking out her compact and fixing her runaway eyeliner.

The drive home is just as silent as the drive over, only this time I switch off the radio.

"I love you," I tell her. "You're the best mom."

She smiles weakly. "Love you too."

Inside, Casey and Dad are playing cards. But they lay their hands flat on the table when my mom sinks into her chair and catches them up on the heartbreaking convo that came out of my follow-up appointment.

"Justin might have been epileptic, too," she says. "The doctor said it's possible his drowning was from a seizure."

That sentence was so unexpected both my dad's and sister's mouths open, but no words come out. No sound, no breath, nothing.

"He had some of Arielle's symptoms," Mom says. "The spacing out. The thrashing in his sleep. He fell out of bed a couple times in the months before . . . it happened."

"I remember that," Dad says, his hand flying to his beard.

"Me too," Casey almost whispers.

"We didn't even *think* to worry." Dad cries instantly. He blows his nose in a tissue from the box on the coffee table. "God, if we had taken him to a doctor—"

"Stop, Dad," Casey says in a wet voice. "Please, don't do that. You can't 'what if' everything now."

"I can't help it." Dad buries his face in his palms.

I still can't swallow this reality, here.

A huge wave of sadness—one so big it's practically a sea heaving invisibly in me—takes over and I join the crying party, too, remembering the day he was pulled from the water, re-membering not understanding why he drowned when he was such a good swimmer.

A seizure.

Of course.

And the ghost flying out of the milk thing—was that just a hallucination related to his messed up temporal lobe, like me and the skeleton girl?

So many feelings rattle through me. Guilt, for one. As in, if my brother and I had the same disease, why am I alive and why is he dead? How is that fair? And fear. Fear remembering how many times I've swum out into the ocean or been alone in a pool with no one around—I could have just as easily drowned. But most of all, I'm heartbroken. He's dead and now we have a glimmer as to why, but it's ten-plus years too late. It's hopeless information that opens up that old wound again in a newer and rawer way.

"There's nothing we could have done," my mom says. "It wasn't our fault."

We hug and cry together, the four of us—we wet each other's shoulders and squeeze tight. And after a while, a new feeling rises from the bottomless sadness: relief. We catch our breath. We wipe our eyes. We comfort each other by repeating the same truths—there was no way to know this back then, it wasn't our fault, it's time to let go . . . and at least I'm here. At least I survived.

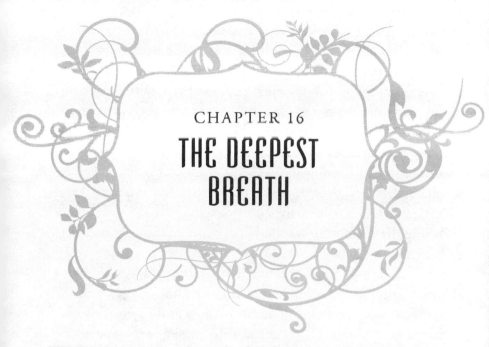

CHAPTER 16
THE DEEPEST BREATH

Each Thanksgiving, the fam gathers around the same glass-topped table with a turkey that Dad spends hours obsessing over. Mom buys the same boxed stuffing and canned cranberry sauce and Casey mashes the potatoes (and never forgets to over-salt them). I make a pumpkin pie from the recipe on the canned pumpkin. None of that is different this year, but one glaring thing is: there's no fifth plate of food served up for Justin. When I ask my mom about it, in shock—I mean, this ritual has gone on for ten years—she just swallows and says, "I think it's time to let it go." My dad rubs her arm. Casey stares at the spot where his plate would be and nods. And I have to admit, something uncoils in me. It always felt borderline creepy, that heaping plate of food served up to a ghost.

We stuff ourselves until I seriously can barely move my body. Casey busts out Scrabble and kicks my butt and pretends she's not gloating. And then Mom and Dad drink wine and watch football on the couch, playing footsie and flirting in a way that's somehow both super endearing and super gross.

This year, though, I appreciate it more. Because I know Casey's going to be flying back to Cambridge in two days. And I'm remembering my ghost of a brother who used to take up the fifth place at the table. I'm thinking of Tex and what his Thanksgiving must be like tonight, with his sister's spot empty. There's just something about this year that stings with realness, with *be-here*ness. Maybe it was the seizure, but life seems so breakable and fragile lately, and as cheesy as it is, I'm actually feeling the thankfulness today even more than the gluttony. Like, take a picture. I don't ever want things to change. And yet, I know they will—and maybe that's why I love this moment right now. Because it's bound to be lost.

After Mom and Dad go to bed, Casey and I put the board games away and just sit at the table talking quietly. She asks me about guys and at first I'm all tight-lipped about it, but then I admit that I'm kinda-sorta not-officially-or-anything seeing Tex.

"Tex *Dell?*" A shadow passes over her face, and I know the mention of him brought her dead friend back to life for a nanosecond. "How is he?" she asks, and draws a circle on the table with her finger.

"Better. I saw his mom the other day. She said to say hi."

She stares at the curtained window. It's still weird to see my stonewall of a sister fight tears, even though I know she has every reason to cry.

"I just feel so guilty," she says.

"Why?" I ask.

She takes so long to answer, I zone out on the clock's ticking. "For moving on with my life."

"What choice did you have?" I ask.

She looks back at the table and her face is blank, white—and I'm sorry I brought this up. All it takes is one word—*Perdita*—to drain the joy from a room.

"Never mind," I say quickly. "Let's talk about something else."

"It's okay. I'm tired, actually. I have to get my boxes ready for the UPS store tomorrow anyway," Casey says, getting up.

"You're really shipping all of them back?" I ask.

"I feel bad for taking up the only storage closet in the living room," she says.

Casey crosses to the closet. Chewing a fingernail, she stares at her tower of boxes in there. I get up, knowing our conversation is over and I should leave her alone. But that little-sister feeling floods back, like when I was a kid and used to follow her everywhere—a fascination that makes me want to stand and watch her do nothing at all. So I lean on the couch and say, "Casey?"

"Hmmm?"

"I opened one of your boxes," I tell her, a little guilty. "Please don't be mad."

She rolls her eyes. "God, you snoop. I knew you'd steal my stuff. I should have locked it all up." I swear we're about to get in a typical fight where she gets paranoid that I'm a "little klepto," out to ransack everything she owns. But then her face softens and she just yawns. "Whatever." She takes a box off the top and puts it on the ground, sitting next to it. "Do we have any permanent markers?"

"I saw something in there," I say quietly.

Casey doesn't even blink. My sister, the statue.

"Those binders?" I say, like a question, because a part of me still can't believe that they're really in there.

She doesn't answer, doesn't move, doesn't even swallow. After a frozen moment, she just says, softly, "They're not mine."

"Whose are they?"

"A friend's," she says.

"Which friend?"

The look on her face is so unfamiliar, there's not even a word in my vocabulary that fits a description to reach for. And then I realize what it is—fear. My sister, hunched below me, is *afraid*.

"Perdita?" I ask.

She *pffft*s. "Yeah, right. No."

"Who, then?" I ask. "Emily?"

My sister was not exactly Miss Popularity. It doesn't take long to go through her friends list.

"God, Arielle, you are so nosy," she says flatly. "I'm getting rid of them. Can you please just forget you saw that and go to bed? I'm too tired to explain everything to you, and really, it's not your business anyway."

That tone in her voice, like my presence is so exhausting, makes me think that maybe things haven't changed at all. I'm still the annoying little sister who won't leave her alone.

"Sorry," I say. "Never mind. Good night."

"'Night," she says.

I tiptoe away, leaving her staring at the box in front of her with the expression of a zombie.

I go to my room and climb into bed. One bonus is, these days, there's no need to record myself anymore. Because I believe in seizures more than I believe in ghosts. Also, since starting the meds, I've found it easier to sleep—I don't know if it's the drowsiness symptom the label warned me about, or if I'm just not afraid of seeing things the way I was before. But still, I lie in the dark for a while thinking about the conversation with Casey in the living room. I think about how she denied it, and how I immediately believed her—I know my sister wouldn't cheat. And she said they weren't Perdita's. She didn't answer me, though, when I asked about Emily, so it seems obvious to me that they're Emily's. But if they are, why does my sister have them at all?

The questions won't let me drift off, so I turn my lamp on (my wonky, still half-broken lamp) and grab my computer. I don't know what compels me, exactly, but I search for Emily on Facebook.

The first thing I notice when I click on her name is that Casey's right—she looks like a totally different human. I mean, I thought Chloe did a one-eighty, but Emily is unrecognizable. She's lost weight, dyed her hair jet black, ditched the glasses, and has huge bangs. The second thing I notice is that we have no mutual friends, which seems super weird. We always had one—Casey. So she and Casey aren't friends anymore.

Then why is my sister guarding Emily's leather binders full of teachers' secret tests, if they're not even friends? Makes the whole thing even weirder.

You have to understand, months ago, just *months* ago, Emily and Casey were all over Facebook in pictures together. School events. Photo-booth snapshots from the burger joint downtown. They double-dated at prom together. I click on Emily's photos and go backward from her jet-haired profile picture, watching a jerky transformation as she bloats back to the size she was originally and goes brunette again, her glasses reappearing, and I stop on a graduation photo where she and my sister are hugging.

Friendships can wither and die in six months' time.

I go forward again through Emily's photos—from graduation, to a picture by the ocean where she's with Casey, to a selfie of her and Casey on a plane with way-too-excited faces, to a picture of Emily in front of a building that looks like it's a dorm, probably at Harvard, to a bunch of pictures in the mirror—suddenly black-haired, gradually thinner, no glasses, bright lipstick, and finally, her newest profile pic, an up-close picture she appears to have taken herself with her head on a pillow. Trying to be sexy or something—which, if you know Emily, is weird and kind of gross.

That's when I notice the little dull something shining.

Her necklace. That one, hanging around her neck.

The silver heart.

"No," I say aloud.

I zoom in on the picture and squint—and sure enough, it is. My lungs forget how to work for a sec; my mouth hangs.

It is a tiny, silver human heart with little veins and all.

Not only that—oh the sickness, the stomach-to-throat sickness I feel when I see it—there's a tiny, hot-pink safety pin hanging down on one side. Yes, the safety pin I gave Perdita the day before she died, to help fasten the necklace back around her neck.

"Holy shit," I say.

My hand is shaking as I go backward in time through her photos again and zoom, zoom, zoom.

Pictures in the mirror? She's wearing the necklace.

Standing in front of the dorm? She's wearing the necklace.

Making a scary-happy clown face next to my sister on the plane? *She's wearing the freaking necklace.*

I shut my computer and think for a long time. I remember the night before Perdita died, when I found her necklace on the floor and got that thought-I saw-a-ghost feeling (that was probably a complex partial seizure, though I had no idea then). I relive her coming back and looking for it, so distraught she thought she lost it—it meant a lot to her. She hadn't taken it off in years. It was custom-made just for her. She would *never* have given it to Emily.

The only way Emily could have that necklace is if she pried it from Perdita's dead, cold neck.

Gulp.

I'm so bothered I get up to see if I can talk to Casey about this. But when I step into the hallway, the house is dark, and I can hear her snoring.

Back in my room, I sit on my bed. My body feels light and strange; my ears ring a little bit. I swallow, thinking, am I really about to have a seizure? On all these meds, right now? But it's not a seizure. No. It's bigger than that.

I glance at my mirror, and see myself on my bed. But guess what? I'm not alone. There's a pale-skinned girl behind me, real as day, in a leather jacket. She stands there and smiles a small, sad, pink-lipped smile.

"Perdita," I almost choke.

"Thanks," she says, her voice clear as a bell.

"For what?" I whisper.

She doesn't blink, doesn't move an inch.

"It was Emily," I say. "I know it was."

I turn behind me, expecting to see her there—but my room is blank. When I whip around to look in the mirror again, she's already gone.

My pulse thunders. There's so much I wanted to say to her. So many questions I'd have loved to ask. But most of all, it's relief that floods me right now. That she's real. That I'm right. That people, when they die, are never really dead. I just had proof of it—and it had nothing to do with neurons misfiring.

I remember my conversation with Tex that first time we were in Perdita's room as we stared at her jacket, and remember what Perdita apparently thought—that people live on in the things they leave behind, or "a ghost that can't move," as Tex referred to them. Jackets and patches and silver necklaces.

"Thank *you*," I whisper to the nothing the air pretends to be. "Don't worry. She won't get away with this."

I crawl into bed.
I watch the room, quiet, not moving.
And believe me, I don't sleep.

I lie awake for most of the night. The point that bothers me the most is that picture of my sister and Emily on the plane, where they're smiling and taking a selfie together, I'm guessing, the first time they flew back east to school. Emily was wearing the necklace then. And, what, my sister didn't notice? I just can't make any sense of this.

When light finally comes—the night was a painful forever—I get up and think about going and talking to my sister, but I can hear my family eating breakfast out there and they're all debating some Black Friday sale. I hear my dad say they should just let me sleep, and then the door slams and everything's quiet. When I tiptoe out to the living room, the apartment's empty. I stare at the couch, at the folded blanket and pillow where my sister slept. My heart is a mallet in my chest—its pounding aches.

The decision makes itself in an instant.

Sometimes, you just know the right thing to do. There's no use in arguing with yourself anymore.

There was that number in the paper and in the article posted online for anonymous tips. When I go back to my room, I look up the article with the phone number in it and grab my phone. There's a text for me from Tex. It was sent late last night.

Hang out this weekend?

I ignore the text and dial the number.

Riiiing, riiiing, riiiing. Then, "This is Detective Lopez."

And I take the deepest breath.

CHAPTER 17

BEFORE AND AFTER

DETECTIVE LOPEZ is the farthest cry from my idea of a cop: soft-spoken, super sweet, and mostly, just a listener. I tell him everything I know—except who I am. He asks if I'd be comfortable letting him write down my name, since I saw Perdita the day before she died and she was wearing the necklace, but I say no. He asks if Emily is in town right now and I say I don't know, but that a lot of college students are home for the holiday. At the end of the call, he thanks me so sincerely and says I did the right thing by calling in. When I hang up, I look at my phone and can't believe the whole conversation took less than seven minutes.

My hands are still shaking.

Mom and Dad come back this afternoon with smiles and ice cream. Usually I'd be like, hell yes! But today I just want to be left alone in my room.

"Are you sure you're okay?" Dad asks suspiciously, standing in the doorway. He's wearing a shirt that says *I hate T-shirts with funny slogans on them.* "What part of 'triple chocolate chip' did you not understand?"

"I'm still bloated from yesterday."

"Suit yourself," Dad says, waving a spoon at me.

"Where's Casey?"

"A detective called and wanted to talk to her." He shrugs. "We dropped her off at the station. Your mom bought you some new pajamas, by the way."

I sit up slowly. Although the pajamas pique my interest, that's not the part that grabbed me about what he just said. "She's . . . talking to a detective?"

"Yeah," he says.

He doesn't seem fazed by this info.

"Well, if you change your mind about chocolate-chocolate-chocolate, you know where to find it. Unless I finish it first."

He closes the door.

I lie back in bed, wanting to gag on the nothing in my stomach.

My sister's at the detective's. I don't have a good feeling about this.

By dinnertime, Casey's still not home. Mom, Dad, and I eat T-day leftovers at the table. Well, actually, I pick at mine—I still don't have an appetite. The past few hours have been eons. Why is my sister talking to the police? Is it my fault, because I called in this morning? I keep staring at the clock while Mom and Dad bicker about whether they should or shouldn't have bought that vacuum at the Black Friday sale today. Casey's been gone at least three hours. Then my mom's phone rings and she gets up.

"Hey, Case." Pause. "Wait—slow down, slow down. What?" Pause. "Casey, *slow down*."

I watch my mom's face lose all expression and color in the time it takes to snap your fingers. She walks immediately to the living room and sits down, ear to phone, listening.

"Oh my God," I hear her say.

I feel the blood draining from my own body at this point. My throat shrinks up as I put my fork on my plate with a horrid clatter and I understand what's happening.

"What is going on?" Dad asks me, putting his napkin down. He looks like someone punched him.

"Casey—Casey, you need to take a breath, okay? You're not going to jail."

GOING TO JAIL??

"I'm calling someone," Mom says. "Don't say anything else. Stay there. I'll be there in a few minutes."

Dad stands up so fast his chair falls down behind him as he scrambles to the living room.

"What happened?" he asks my mom.

I just sit at the table, numb, staring at the half-eaten plates, wondering if I've ruined everyone's lives.

"Today *Emily* confessed to . . . murdering Perdita," she says. "The police brought her in for questioning and they asked for a swab—and she just confessed."

She speaks the words so oddly, like it's not English.

"*Emily?*" my dad shouts. "No."

"I don't understand, exactly." You can hear phlegm in my mother's voice. "But Emily's trying to pull Casey into it somehow."

My stomach flips.

"This is crazy," Dad says. "This is a mistake. She's lying."

"Of course she's lying. But Casey's hysterical. The police are trying to say Casey can be charged as an accessory after the fact."

A nightmare curtain closes on us then; a dark cloud inhabits the apartment and I suck that dark cloud into my lungs and it becomes a part of me.

I hear my parents put their coats on, grab car keys, and slam the door behind them.

Casey. My sister. *What has she done?*

The silence is so long and sharp, a river of knives in the air, me feeling so awful and hating myself for making this happen. A car alarm somewhere, far away, goes on and then off again.

I get up and stand in my room, stunned, staring at my unmade bed where I made the call earlier. Staring at my own reflection, which looks like a complete stranger's. I put my hand to my throat and squeeze for a minute, thinking if this is a nightmare, that might wake me up.

Not so lucky.

This moment—right now—this here, this is change swallowing us like a tsunami. This is change coming uninvited and tearing our house down, yanking my sister from us, aging my parents years in mere minutes. My phone is buzzing on the dresser. It's Tex. I watch the phone dance and realize there are tears hurrying down my face. Some invisible beast came and ripped my ribcage open. I want to die right now. I want to disappear. Or no—I want to go backward, backward; I want to shrink into what I was a few months ago, or a year ago, before the hatchet of truth came, before it separated everything that was one life into Before and After.

CHAPTER 18

AND A WISH

T HE TRUTH COMES IN PIECES, over days, then weeks.
Casey doesn't go to jail—her lawyer helps her make some
kind of deal since she'll testify against Emily in Emily's trial.
The whole ordeal is so complicated I barely understand it myself, but I'll try to explain it as best I can.

Here goes.

At the end of Casey's junior year (my freshman year), when
Emily and my sister became super close, and Perdita drifted
away, Emily worked in the office at school during sixth period.
Her job was mostly filing boring papers for teachers and ad-
ministrators, and answering phones. Apparently no one noticed
that now and then she slipped off with teachers' files—master
tests, midterms, finals that were stored in the school's filing

system—and made copies for herself. Emily and Casey were dead set on Ivy League schools, and even though they had the right SAT scores, apparently Emily was worried about their grades in AP classes. They were overwhelmed with extracurricular stuff—yearbook, swimming, debate team. So Emily convinced Casey to use the tests to boost their chances of getting into top schools in the last difficult semesters. It's still hard for me to fathom that my sister cheated. Some things you just have to learn to accept—one of them is that everyone you know, even your siblings, even your best friends, has the ability to shock the hell out of you now and then.

They used these copied tests at the end of their junior year and the first semester of their senior year. But when Casey told Perdita about what she'd been doing, Perdita threatened to tell the school—unless Emily and Casey paid her to keep quiet. My sister drained her savings, and so did Emily. Perdita took the cash and didn't tell anyone about the cheating and they all graduated, no problem. Win-win-win, right?

But at the end of the summer, when Casey and Emily were getting ready to leave for Harvard, Perdita threatened them both again, repeatedly, saying she would tell the school everything if they didn't pay her more money. Casey thought she was jealous. Emily claimed she was greedy. I wonder if it was just Perdita's sick way of trying to keep her friend from moving away from her.

So after Perdita's latest threat, which exploded into a three-way argument in Casey's room, Emily agreed to meet Perdita at the lake that night to talk her out of blackmailing them again. What happened wasn't planned. They started fighting. It escalated quickly. Perdita scratched Emily with her fingernails and Emily grabbed Perdita by the hair and dunked her head in the water "until she was quiet." Then, for reasons I will never understand, Emily took the necklace and wore it thereafter like a prize. And if she hadn't, we never would have known the truth.

That necklace detail? Left by an anonymous tipster. No one knows who. Not even Casey.

My sister wasn't there. My sister had nothing to do with Perdita's drowning—at least we have that much. Emily told her what happened the next day, and told her if she got caught, she would tell the police everything—including the cheating and Casey's involvement. Casey's chances of going to school would be nil. All Casey wanted was to get out of Velero. Perdita was already dead. Emily said it was an accident. So Casey didn't call the police.

Casey knew, and she didn't tell anyone.

A week after Casey officially moves back into the apartment—too ashamed to face Harvard, and she'd probably be booted anyway, since the story exploded in the papers—I stop going to school. I don't know how these things happen, but everyone and their dog finds out that Casey had something to do with Perdita's death. People talk. And I catch her shame like a contagious disease. That's about when Tex stops trying to message me on Facebook and starts texting me nonstop. I miss him like a hole but feel so mortified by what my sister did to his sister, all I can think to do is vanish quietly from his life. Which is terrible and I know it. Which makes me feel even worse.

Chloe says that for the most part, Tex stopped showing up to school, too.

Every day, my sister's name is mentioned in the same articles as Emily's, and Emily's senior portrait is blown up on the front

page of the *Velero Voice* with words like TEEN KILLER above
her forehead in block letters. It's warped—it's beyond bizarre.

Time kind of just . . . stops for a while. Feelings dry up.
Chloe brings my schoolwork home to me, my parents take me
to the doctor to adjust my meds, but otherwise I just stay in
my room watching TV. And soon it's been more than a week,
and then it's been a month, and before I know it the season's
changed again and I realize I've done nothing but lie around
the apartment in a daze. I haven't even posted on Facebook.

Now I know what it feels like to be a ghost.

I'm not going to lie—I've thought some terrible things since
all this started. Thoughts that are so weird, so foreign, they
don't even feel like they belong in my own brain. I've thought
about getting blotto on drugs I've never even tried. I've thought
about running away, dyeing my hair, and changing my name.
I've thought about becoming a bum and sleeping on park
benches, because I hate feeling trapped in this apartment with
Casey on the couch in the living room and my parents going
grayer every time I look at them. But I do nothing.

I do nothing like a freaking professional.

We're halfway through the second semester when Emily
pleads guilty for a reduced sentence. *Guilty.* Casey takes me to
Starbucks one morning and tells me the news. She reports it
all so matter-of-factly, with a faraway look in her eyes, as we
sip Frappuccinos. Emily was charged with manslaughter. She's
getting ten years in prison. She could be out in five, on good
behavior.

Five years.

That's *it.*

The news makes me so sick I have to remind myself not to
regurgitate my sugar-coffee.

And Casey's officially off the hook. Although she's still a
cheater and the friend of a murderer, and everyone in town

knows it. Like, for instance, Raffi took one look at us walking in today and turned around to the espresso machine. You think I'm depressed? Besides this Starbucks date, Casey seriously hasn't left the house except to go to lawyer appointments since this all started. She's wearing Uggs and pajama pants in public.

"I'm thinking of moving to San Diego," Casey says.

We sip our drinks and stare out the window, at a woman holding a baby, kissing the baby's head. The woman is young and blond. When I look back at Casey, there are tears brightening her eyes.

"I'm so sorry," she says.

I shrug. "I know."

"Believe me, this isn't what I wanted. I never wanted any of this."

This is the first time, since the trial started, that Casey has actually talked to me directly about what happened.

"If something like that had happened to Chloe," I say, "there's no way I could have kept it a secret."

"What if everything had been resting on it?" she asks, voice quivering. "And you couldn't bring her back anyway?"

"I don't think I'm the one whose forgiveness you should be asking."

Her eyes fill up again. She squeezes my hand over the tabletop. I let her. At the green counter, I see Raffi staring with a blank expression. And you know what? I don't care.

I miss my life the way it was before. Before Emily's manslaughter charges, before the threats of my sister's arrest, before I started suspecting my sister could be involved in a murder. Before epilepsy, before my seizures, before meds that make me moody and tired, before I saw ghosts. Before Chloe got a boyfriend and bleached her hair, before the school year started, before my sister went away to school, before Perdita drowned. Before we moved. Before I fell in love. Before, beautiful Before.

It doesn't matter anymore.

I don't know what's going to become of me. My sister took the train to San Diego last week, but I'm still here in Velero. I miss my parents even though they're a room away from me, but when I join them for dinner or hang out in the living room, I realize I miss another version of them. The Before version. I mean, when I tell this version of my parents I'm thinking about testing out of school, they tell me they support my decision. That's crazy! They never would have said something like that six months ago. It's all backward and upside down.

The days are getting longer and warmer. This evening, the sky is twilight-silver and smeared with cotton candy clouds. The moon lurks behind the fading sunset. I put on a jacket and decide to start walking. I don't take anything with me but my keys and phone. I walk down our tree-lined street with the dark, set-back buildings and lamplit windows, head up the boulevard, and pass Trinkets and a laundromat and a Taco Bell. I go over the overpass and stop and watch the cars flashing below me, speeding to who knows where, and I wish I were there and not here.

I keep walking. Down, over the overpass, toward the supermarket and hardware store, past all that, to the left, and I realize I'm just stepping one foot in front of the other, zombie-style. I'm headed toward my old house.

It's not completely night yet, but the moon is fuller than I swear it's ever been. Like pregnant full. So yellow it burns. I follow it to my old street, where I turn. My calves burn—I haven't walked this far in months—but it feels good. And my quick heartbeat, and the beads of sweat, they feel good, too. To the left, the dark curtain of trees that flank the lake. To the right, the row of houses so familiar I ache.

I stand in front of my house. My house! It *was* my house. I ran through sprinklers every summer on this lawn. I fell off that roof when I was eleven and broke my arm. My dad's car used to be parked right there, and Mom's right beside it. Now there's some unfamiliar van and a couple bikes, wind chimes where there didn't used to be wind chimes, and someone had the gall to cut the maple out of the front yard. It hurts to look at.

I turn around and cross the street, walking the dirt path next to the lake. Right here, right where I'm standing in the entrance—this was where the crowd gathered early that morning when Perdita's body was found. My sister was upstairs sleeping.

I turn right and walk through the entrance, up the path that opens between the trees. After a short distance, the trees thin and the lake appears to my right, shining midnight blue beneath the darkening sky. Down the slope, right down there near the reeds and rushes, is where her body was found. I watched it from the brush near the road.

I walk down the slope, passing the unused lifesaver in its wooden case, and stop suddenly when I realize two things. Number one, there's a chain-link fence now at the lake's edge where there didn't use to be; and number two, someone's standing against it, looking out at the water. Someone whose outline I recognize in a breath, even though he's turned around, even though it's almost dark.

It's Tex.

I almost turn away. Not Tex! *Anyone* but Tex. My heart is in my neck and I'm choking on it. I look terrible, I'm sure, in these yoga pants and T-shirt that I practically live in. My hair hasn't seen a brush in days—although why I'm focusing on these details is beyond me. My worries are much deeper than all that. I think about sneaking away, so he never knows I was here. But I'm paralyzed. And just when I think I might have it in me to jog away and pretend I never saw him, he turns around and stares at me. The look on his face when he recognizes me is like I just stuck him with a knife.

"What the *hell*?" he finally says.

"Hi," is all I can think to say.

"Why are you here?"

"I don't know. I've been out walking."

He has more facial hair than he did when I last saw him. He, too, could stand to put on a few pounds. His hair looks darker, greasier, longer. It almost touches his shoulders now.

"Did you come here to find me or something?"

"No," I say. "I just ended up here."

His face goes blank. When I imagined us meeting again, I expected him to be angry, hurt. Bitterness and sharp words. I didn't expect his eyes to lock with mine like this, for him to just stand there so calmly. I remember last summer when he first stared at me like the Girl Made of Glass. I want that moment back. He watches me now like he's thinking of other things, things that aren't here.

"That's really weird," he says.

He turns back to look at the lake, grabbing the fence with his hands.

"The fence is new," I say.

"Pretty retarded, don't you think?" he asks. "Like a fence is going to stop some chick from murdering some other chick."

The word *murdering* slices through the air.

Crickets cheep. An owl cries.

"I still can't believe it," I say quietly.

"Yeah."

Words seem so weak. Pebbles in a sea.

"You didn't have to, like, drop off the face of the planet," he says.

I cross my arms, a breeze chilling me. "What was I supposed to do?"

"You were supposed to be my friend, right?" he asks.

Girlfriend, actually, I don't say.

"I'm still your friend," I say.

"Right."

He doesn't even turn around to look at me.

"Do you hate me?" I ask. "It's okay if you do. I mean, you *should* hate me. I can't believe Casey knew—I just still can't believe any of it."

"I do hate you," he says simply.

Ouch.

It still hurts to be right.

"Yeah," I say, after a moment. "How can you not?"

He turns around, leans back on the fence, and faces me.

"Oh, I don't hate you because of what Casey did or didn't do," he says, staring at me, his lips a straight line. "I hate you because you just *left* me. You just ditched me like an asshole. You didn't even return my texts."

My throat closes up a little.

"I can't hate you because of what happened between our sisters. But I can totally hate you for being a shitty friend."

"I'm sorry," I whisper.

He steps toward me, and I don't know what it is in his eyes. It's something I've never seen before. He reaches his arms out and grabs my arms, hard, and shakes me.

"You didn't even care," he says. "You think this is all about you?"

The world around me quakes and blurs, he shakes me so hard. My teeth chatter.

"I'm sorry," I cry.

His fingers grasp me harder, pinching my arms. He pushes me backward and I struggle. I realize I'm crying, my eyes are stinging, and I'm having a hard time talking. I'm afraid of him, of how loud his voice is—I've never heard him waver like that—and the tears streaking down his face and neck.

"You wouldn't even answer my *texts*," he says. "You wouldn't even give me one single word."

I wonder if he would hurt me, really hurt me, and in a weird way I almost want him to. I'm so mixed up. I'm girl-shaped hurt. Everywhere, from deep in my bones to the stupid tears on my face, it all pains. I go limp, and his fingers dig into my upper arms even more.

"You don't even care that I care," he says.

"I do," I say. "I was ashamed."

"Your sister knew my sister was murdered," he says suddenly, and lets go of my arms. "And didn't tell *anyone*."

My arm throbs in the places he gripped a moment ago. I rub them and rub my tears on the back of my hand.

We wipe our faces and those words hang in the air like a strange doom. We don't even blink. We stare and I see that he's staring far into me, farther than my tears or my stupid T-shirt and yoga pants, farther than Casey's sister and farther than the girl who was almost his girlfriend for a minute. I don't know what he's seeing. But I see far into him, too. I see his goodness, there, his hurt, his guilt, his loneliness; I recognize myself.

That's when he reaches for me, quickly, reaches his arms around my neck.

He holds me, and I hold him, and we go still. I can hear an airplane somewhere above our heads. His smell pierces me. I miss him. How I miss him. I rest my chin on his shoulder and touch his hair and I feel, for a moment, like he and I are going backward. To a peaceful place. To before the death and secrets and pain.

"I just thought, how could we ever be together now?" I ask quietly. "After everything? How could we even be friends?"

"My family hates your sister," he says. "My mom told me she wouldn't even want you over, after what Casey did, and after how you stopped talking to me."

I pull away. "I deserve that."

But he pulls me in tighter. "I don't give a shit what my mom thinks. I want you," he says into my shoulder. "Let's go somewhere where no one knows us."

"This town is too small."

"I would go if you wanted, Arielle. Just say the word." He pulls back and stares at me. God, he is so beautiful. Those lips—I could get lost in the mere sight of his lips for hours. "Say it."

I look to the right, through the chainlink fence and at the black shine of the lake water. It's totally dark now.

"Say it," he says louder, like he's begging me to.

I could go. I can imagine it. I could hop on the back of his motorcycle and we could ride to another state. Somewhere snowy in the winter, somewhere nestled in pine trees, some small town where no one knows who the Delaneys or the Dells are. We could get jobs, GEDs. We could start a life together. We could be so happy.

"Wouldn't that be crazy?" I ask.

"No," he says. "It makes perfect sense."

I stare at him. "Where would we go?"

"Wherever we feel like," he says.

I think about change, that destructive giant who never asks permission. For once in my life, I'd like change to be my doing—for change to be something that's a joy, an adventure, and not a storm or a horror.

"When?" I ask, my pulse racing, adrenaline bursting.

He kisses me—a quick, soft kiss—and my legs turn to jelly.

"Tonight?" he says. "Let's just do it. Let's go pack our bags and we'll go, before we have time to chicken out."

"I'd have to sneak home to grab my stuff," I say, the excitement fireworking in my veins as the words come out and it starts becoming real. "Some cash and clean clothes."

"Really? We're really going to do this?"

He breaks into a smile and we hug. I bury my face in his shoulder. I can't believe my good luck—to find him here, of all places, and now, of all times—and he still loves me. And we're going to leave this place and not look back. Start over. It's going to be perfect; it's going to be a movie.

"You'll drive us on your motorcycle?" I ask as we hurry up the bank, to the main path.

"It's broken," he says. "We'll have to take a Greyhound."

"But to where?" I ask.

We powerwalk toward the entrance, holding hands.

"Who cares," he says. "We'll pack and meet at the station and decide then."

We stop and stare in the dark, on the sidewalk outside the lake entrance. Across the street from my old house. I can't believe this is happening—I can't believe this is my life, that everything's about to change for the better.

"Okay," I say. "We'll meet at the Greyhound station."

"In an hour," he says.

"An hour," I echo.

"I love you so much," he says.

We kiss again—this time a long, sloppy, hungry kiss. I'm lost in it. I don't want to stop, but he pulls away.

"Hurry," he says.

"Okay."

We part ways. He runs toward his house and I run toward mine. I have a longer run—looping past the supermarket, up the freeway overpass, down again, past the Taco Bell and Trinkets and streets and more streets, and finally I'm in front of my parents' apartment building, catching my breath as I head up the stairs. I'm thinking of the future. I can taste it and it's me and Tex and a little house with a motorcycle parked out front. It's a place our families have never been and where our sisters don't exist. I'll sleep with him every night under sheets that are ours. We'll be together; we'll be new.

I slide the key into my front door and gently unlock it, tiptoe inside in the dark, and slip into my room. I put the light on, grab a backpack, and start packing. I find some cash stashed in my sock drawer and a ring that might be worth something. I pack some clothes. It only takes a minute. I turn off the light and close the door behind me and stand in the hallway. I stare at the pictures on the wall. At Casey's senior picture. She's smiling and staring right at me. Back when she was happy, when she had her life ahead of her and nothing to run away from. My sister, the cheater, the friend who kept her lips sealed about a murder. Her face looks like mine.

I should go. Go! Get to the Greyhound station. It's a half-hour walk from here. But I can't move. I'm frozen.

Behind the closed door, I can hear my mom crying.

"Honey," my dad just keeps saying. "Honey."

"How did we let this happen?" Mom weeps.

My dad's crying with her now. I stand, staring at their door, and immediately catch their sadness, too. I snivel into my hands. Big, rock-me sobs. The sadness in me grows. It swells so gigantic it seems to spill out of me. It seems to fill the whole house; it seeps into the air; it becomes the whole world. And it's not just for them; it's not just for my parents, there, crying behind the door.

It's for me.

It's because I know I can't escape this sadness by hopping on a bus and going to a town where no one knows my name. I can't go anywhere. I can't do that to my parents. They already lost one daughter this year, in a way. And they lost their son a decade ago. I mean, really.

Slack and wiping my face, I turn around and go back into my room. I flip the light on and put my backpack on the ground. I sit on the bed. I take out my phone.

Listen, I text Tex. *I just can't go yet.*

I listen to the hum in my ears. Finally, my phone lights up and buzzes.

I knew u were gonna say that, is all he says.

I mean it, I text. *Just give it time. We'll start over. We'll go somewhere no one knows us.*

I press a finger to the pang in my chest, look at my phone again, and reread the last text I sent him. I wipe my cheeks, breathe deep. There's a ghostly ache in my gut I know isn't going to go away—at least not anytime soon. I meant what I texted him. The future's still a dream.

Tell me . . . what's the difference, anyway, between a lie and a wish?

Huge thanks to the following people, without whom this book would not be a thing:

My amazing agent and expert advice-giver Claire Anderson-Wheeler, who not only championed the business of this book, but helped shape the story into what it is now.

My editor Jackie and everyone at Merit Press for the beautiful design and the hard work it takes to make a book real.

The best best friend I could ask for (and impromptu publicist), Ramona Itule.

Eliza Smith, the smartest ghost-lover I know.

Melissa Dale for making me look better in pictures.

Austen Rachlis for reading and giving feedback on the earliest version of this story.

Mom, Dad, Matt, Jackson, and Micaela, my favorite characters on earth.

My husband Jamie, the listener I love more than words.

My daughter Roxanna, who was born the same incredible week *Perdita* found a home.